Brander Matthews

Outlines in local color

Brander Matthews

Outlines in local color

ISBN/EAN: 9783743309074

Manufactured in Europe, USA, Canada, Australia, Japa

Cover: Foto ©Andreas Hilbeck / pixelio.de

Manufactured and distributed by brebook publishing software
(www.brebook.com)

Brander Matthews

Outlines in local color

[Page 291

GREETINGS FROM THE PROMENADE

Outlines in Local Color

BY

BRANDER MATTHEWS

ILLUSTRATED

BY W. T. SMEDLEY

NEW YORK AND LONDON
HARPER & BROTHERS PUBLISHERS
1898

By BRANDER MATTHEWS.

"When I came to my chamber I writ down these minutes; but was at a loss what instruction I should propose to my readers from the enumeration of so many insignificant matters and occurrences; and I thought it of great use, if they could learn with me to keep their minds open to gratification, and ready to receive it from anything it meets with."

—STEELE, in "*The Spectator*," *August* 11, 1712.

CONTENTS

ILLUSTRATIONS

An Interview with Miss Marlenspuyk

IT was a chill day early in January, and at four in the afternoon a gray sky shut in the city, like the cylindrical background of a cyclorama. Now and then a wreath of steam chalked itself on the slate-colored horizon; and across the river, far over to the westward, there was a splash of pink, sole evidence of the existence of the sun, which no one had seen for twenty-four hours.

As Miss Marlenspuyk turned the corner of the side street she stood still for a moment, looking down on the long Riverside Drive and on the mighty Hudson below, flowing sluggishly beneath its shield of ice. She had long passed the limit of threescore years and ten, and she had been an indefatigable traveller; and as she gazed, absorbing the noble beauty of the splendid scene, unsurpassable in any other city she had ever visited, she was glad that she was a New-Yorker born and bred, and that it was her privilege to dwell where a vision like this was to be had for the asking. But while she looked lovingly up and down the solemn stream the wind sprang up again, and fluttered her gray curls and blew her wrappings about her.

Two doors above the corner where Miss Marlenspuyk was standing a striped awning stretched its convolutions across the sidewalk and up the irregular stone steps, and thrust itself into the doorway at the top of the stoop. A pretty young girl, with a pleasantly plump figure and with a dash of gold in her fair hair, passed through this twisting canvas tunnel just ahead of Miss Marlenspuyk; and when the door of the house was opened to admit them they entered together, the old maid and the young girl.

The house was illuminated as though it were already night; the curtains were drawn, and the lamps, with their fantastically extravagant shades of fringed silk, were all alight. The atmosphere was heavy with the perfume of flowers, which were banked up high on the mantel-pieces and the tables, while thick festoons of smilax were pendent from all the gas-fixtures and over all the mirrors. Palms stood in the corners and in the fireplaces; and at one end of the hall they were massed as a screen, through which glimpses could be caught of the bright uniforms of the Hungarian band.

In the front parlor, before a broad table on which there were a dozen or more beautiful bouquets tied with bows of ribbon, and under a bower of solid ropes of smilax, stood the lady of the house with the daughter she was that afternoon introducing to society. The hostess was a handsome, kindly woman, with scarce a gray hair in her thick dark braids. The daughter was, like her mother, kindly also, and also handsome : she was better looking, really, than any of the six or seven pretty girls she had asked to aid her in receiving her mother's friends and acquaintances.

The young woman who had preceded Miss Marlenspuyk into the house happened also to precede her in entering the parlor. The hostess, holding her bunch of orchids in the left hand, greeted the girl pleasantly, but perhaps with a vague hint of condescension.

" Miss Peters, isn't it ?" said the lady of the house, pitching her voice low, but with an effort, as though the habit had been acquired late in life. "So good of you to come on such a nasty day. Mildred, you know Miss Peters ?"

Then the daughter stepped forward and smiled and shook hands with Miss Peters, thus leaving the mother at liberty to greet Miss Marlenspuyk ; and this time there was no trace of condescension in her manner, but rather a faint suggestion of satisfaction.

"Oh. Miss Marlenspuyk," she said, cordially, "this is a pleasure. So good of you to come on such a nasty day."

" It did blow as I came to the top of your hill here," Miss Marlenspuyk returned, "and I'm not as strong as I was once upon a time. I suppose that few of us are as frisky at seventy-five as we were at seventeen."

"I protest," said the hostess; "you don't

look a day older now than when I first met you."

"That's not so very long ago," the old maid answered. "I don't think I've known you more than five or ten years, have I? And five or ten years are nothing to me now. I don't feel any older than I did half a century ago; but as for my looks—well, the least said about them is soonest mended. I never was a good-looker, you know."

"How can you say so?" responded the hostess, absently noting a group of new-comers gathering in the door-way. "Mildred, you know Miss Marlenspuyk?"

"Oh yes, indeed I do," the girl said, heartily, shaking hands with the vivacious old maid.

The young woman with the touch of gold in her light hair was still standing by Mildred's side. Noting this, and seeing the group of new-comers breaking from the door-way and coming towards her, the hostess spoke hastily again.

"Do you know Miss Peters, Miss Marlenspuyk?" she asked. "Well, at all events, Miss Peters ought to know you."

Then she had just time to greet the group of new-comers and to lower her voice again, and to tell them it was so good of them to come on such a nasty day.

The daughter was left talking to Miss Marlenspuyk and Miss Peters, but within a minute her mother called her — "Mildred, you know Mrs. Hitchcock?"

AN AFTERNOON AT HOME

As the group of new-comers pressed forward the old maid with the bright blue eyes, and the young woman with the pleasantly plump figure, fell back a little.

" I've heard so much of you, Miss Marlenspuyk, from my grandfather," began the younger woman.

" Your grandfather !" echoed the elder lady. " Then your father must be a son of Bishop Peters ?"

Little Miss Peters nodded.

" Then your grandfather was a great friend of my younger brother's," Miss Marlenspuyk continued. " They went to school together. I remember the first time I saw the Bishop—it must be sixty years ago — it was the day he was put into trousers for the first time ! And wasn't he proud of them !"

Miss Peters joined Miss Marlenspuyk in laughing at this amusing memory.

Then the old maid asked, " Your father married in the South after the war, didn't he ? Wasn't your mother from Atlanta ?"

" He lived there till mother died : I was bo'n there," said the girl. " I've been No'th only two years now this Christmas."

" I don't suppose you found many of your grandfather's friends left. Nowadays people die so absurdly young," the old maid remarked. " Is your father here this afternoon ?"

" Oh dear no," responded Miss Peters ; " he

has to live in Southe'n Califo'nia for his health.
I'm in New Yo'k all alone."

"I'm sorry for you, my child," said the elder
woman, taking the girl's hand. "I've been alone
myself a great deal, and I know what it means.
But you must do as I did — make friends with
yourself, and cultivate a liking for your own society."

The younger woman laughed lightly, and answered, "But I haven't as cha'ming a companion
as you had."

Miss Marlenspuyk smiled back. "Yes, you
have, my child. I'm not an ill-looking old woman now, I know, but I was a very plain girl; and
I know it isn't good for any one's character to be
conscious that she's almost ugly. But I set out
to make the best of it, and I did. I thought it
likely I should have a good deal of my own society, and so I made friends with this forced ac-
quaintance. Now, I'm very good company for
myself. I'm rarely dull, for I find myself an
amusing companion, and we have lots of inter-
ests in common. And if you choose you can
also cultivate a friendship for yourself. But it
won't be as necessary for you as for me, because
you are a pretty girl, you see. That glint of
gold in your fair hair is really very fetching. And what are you doing here in New York
all alone?"

"I'm writing," Miss Peters replied.

"Writing?" echoed Miss Marlenspuyk.

"My father's in ve'y bad health, as I told you," the younger woman explained, "and I have to suppo't myself. So I write."

"But I don't think I've seen anything signed Peters in the magazines, have I?" asked the old maid.

"Oh, the magazines!" Miss Peters returned—"the magazines! I'm not old enough to have anything in the magazines yet. You have to wait so long for them to publish an article, even if they do accept it. But I get things into the weeklies sometimes. The first time I have a piece printed that I think you'd like, I'll send it to you, if I may."

"I will read it at once and with pleasure," Miss Marlenspuyk declared, cordially.

"I don't sign my own name yet," continued Miss Peters; "I use a pen-name. So perhaps you have read something of mine without knowing it."

"Perhaps I have, my child," said Miss Marlenspuyk. "I shall be on the lookout for you now. It must be delightful to be able to put your thoughts down in black and white, and send them forth to help make the world brighter and better."

Little Miss Peters laughed again, disclosing a fascinating dimple.

"I don't believe I shall ever write anything that will make the world better," she said; "and if I did, I don't believe the editor would take it.

I don't think that is just what editors are after
nowadays—do you? They're on the lookout for
stuff that 'll sell the paper."

"Sad stuff it is, too, most of it," the old maid
declared. "When I was a girl the newspapers
were violent enough, and the editors abused each
other like pickpockets, and sometimes they called
each other out, and sometimes somebody else
horsewhipped them. But the papers then weren't
as silly and as cheap and as trivial as the papers
are now. It seems as though the editors to-day
had a profound contempt for their readers, and
thought anything was good enough for them.
Why, I had a letter from a newspaper last week
—a printed form it was, too—stating that they
were 'desirous of obtaining full and correct information on Society Matters, and would appre-
ciate the kindness if Miss Marlenspuyk would
forward to the Society Editor any information
regarding entertainments she may purpose giving during the coming winter, and the Society
Editor will also be happy to arrange for a full
report when desired.' Was there ever such im-
pudence? To ask me to describe my own dinners, and to give a list of my guests! As though
any lady would do a thing like that!"

"There are ladies who do," ventured Miss
Peters.

"Then they are not what you and I would call
ladies, my child," returned Miss Marlenspuyk.

The face of the Southern girl flushed suddenly,

and she bit her lip in embarrassment. Then she mustered up courage to ask, " I suppose you do not read the *Daily Dial*. Miss Marlenspuyk ?"

" I tried it for a fortnight once," the old maid answered. " They told me it had the most news, and all that. But I had to give it up. Nobody that I knew ever died in the *Dial*. My friends all died in the *Gotham Gazette*."

" The *Gazette* has a larger family circulation," admitted the younger woman.

" Besides." Miss Marlenspuyk continued. " I could not stand the vulgarity of the *Dial*. I'm an old woman now, and I've seen a great deal of the world. but the *Dial* was too much for me. It seemed to be written down to the taste of the half-naked inhabitants of an African kraal."

" Oh," protested the other. " do you really think it is as bad as that ?"

" Indeed I do." the old maid affirmed. " It's worse than that. because the poor negroes wouldn't know better. And what was most offensive, perhaps, in the *Dial* was the unwholesome knowingness of it."

" I see what you mean," said Miss Peters, and again the color rose in her cheeks.

" There was that Lightfoot divorce case." Miss Marlenspuyk went on. " The way the *Dial* dwelt on that was unspeakable. I'm willing to allow that Mrs. Lightfoot was not exactly a nice person ; I'll admit that she may have been divorced more times than she had been married—"

"That's admitting a good deal!" said the young woman, as the elder paused.

" But it is going altogether too far to say that, like Cleopatra, she had the manners of a kitten and the morals of a cat—isn't it ?"

Miss Peters made no response. Her eyes were fixed on the carpet, and her face was redder than ever.

"Of course it isn't likely you saw the article I mean," the old maid continued.

" Yes," the younger responded. " I saw it."

"I'm sorry for that," said Miss Marlenspuyk. " I may be old-fashioned—I suppose I must be at my age—but I don't think that is the kind of thing a nice girl like you should read."

Again Miss Peters made no response.

" I happen to remember that phrase," Miss Marlenspuyk continued, " because the article was signed ' Polly Perkins.' Very likely it was a man who wrote it, after all, but it may have been a woman. And if it was I felt ashamed for her as I read it. How could one woman write of another in that way ?"

" Perhaps the writer was very poor," pleaded Miss Peters.

" That would not be a good reason, and it is a bad excuse," the old maid declared. " Of course I don't know what I should do if I were desperately poor—one never knows. But I think I'd live on cold water and a dry crust sooner than earn my bread and butter that way—wouldn't you ?"

Miss Peters did not answer this direct question. For a moment she said nothing. Then she raised her head, and there was a hint of high resolve in the emphasis with which she said, " It is a mean way to make a living."

Before Miss Marlenspuyk could continue the conversation she was greeted by two ladies who had just arrived. Miss Peters drew back and stood by herself in a corner for a few minutes as the throng in front of her thickened. She was gazing straight before her, but she was not conscious of the people who encompassed her about. Then she aroused herself, and went into the dining-room and had a cup of tea and a thin slice of buttered bread, rolled up and tied with a tiny ribbon. And perhaps fifteen minutes later she found herself in front of the hostess.

She told the hostess that she had had such a very good time. that she didn't know when she had met such very agreeable people, and that she was specially delighted with an old friend of her grandfather's, Miss Marlenspuyk. " Such a very delightful old maid. with none of the flavor of desiccated spinsterhood. She does her own thinking. too. She gave me some of her ideas about modern journalism."

" She is a brilliant conversationalist," said the hostess. " You might have interviewed her."

" Oh. she talked freely enough," Miss Peters responded. " But I could never write her up properly. Besides, I'm thinking of giving up newspaper wo'k."

Three ladies here came towards the hostess, who stepped forward with extended hand, saying, " So good of you to come on such a nasty day." Miss Peters availed herself of the opportunity, and made her escape.

It might be half an hour afterwards when Miss Marlenspuyk, having had her cup of tea and her roll of bread-and-butter, returned to the front parlor in time to overhear a bashful young man take leave of the hostess, and wish the hostess's daughter " many happy returns of the day."

As it happened, there was a momentary stagnation of the flood of guests when Miss Marlenspuyk went up to say farewell, and she had a chance to congratulate the daughter of the house on the success of her coming-out tea.

" Then I must tell you, Miss Marlenspuyk," said the hostess, " that you completely fascinated little Miss Peters."

" She's a pretty little thing," the old maid returned, " with excellent manners. That comes with the blood, I suppose ; she told me she was a granddaughter of the Bishop, you know. She isn't like so many of the girls here, who take what manners they have out of a book. They get them up overnight, but she was born with them. And she has the final sign of breeding, which is so rare nowadays—she listens when her elders are talking."

"Yes," the hostess replied, "Pauline Peters has pleasant manners, for all she is working on a newspaper now."

"On a newspaper?" repeated Miss Marlenspuyk. "She told me she was writing for her living, but she didn't say she was on a newspaper."

"She said something about giving it up as she went out," the hostess remarked; "but I shouldn't think she would, for she has been doing very well. Some of her articles have made quite a hit. You know she is the 'Polly Perkins' of the *Daily Dial?*"

"No," said Miss Marlenspuyk—"no, I didn't know that."

(1895)

A Letter of Farewell

THERE had been a hesitating fall of snow in the morning, but before noon it had turned to a mild and fitful rain that had finally modified itself into a clinging mist as evening drew near. The heavy snow-storm of the last week in January had left the streets high on both sides with banks that thawed swiftly whenever the sun came out again, the water running from them into the broad gutters, and then freezing hard at night, when the cold wind swept across the city. Now, at nightfall, after a muggy day, a sickening slush had spread itself treacherously over all the crossings. The shop-girls going home had to pick their way cautiously from corner to corner under the iron pillars supporting the station of the elevated railroad. Train followed train overhead, each close on the other's heels; and clouds of steam swirled down as the engines came to a full stop with a shrill grinding of the brakes. From the skeleton spans of the elevated road moisture dripped on the cable-cars below, as they rumbled along with their bells clanging sharply when they neared the crossings. The atmosphere was thick with a damp haze; and there was a halo about every

yellow globe in the windows of the bar-rooms at
the four corners of the avenue.   More frequent,
as the dismal day wore to an end, was the hoarse
and lugubrious tooting of the ferryboats in the
East River.

Under the steps of the stairs leading up to
the aërial station of the railroad overhead, an
Italian street vender had wheeled the barrow
whereon he proffered for sale bananas and ap-
ples and nuts.   At one end of this stand was the
cylinder in which he was roasting peanuts, and
which he ground as conscientiously as though
he were turning a hand-organ.   A scant quarter
past six o'clock it might have been, when he
opened his fire-box to throw in a stick or two
more of fuel and to warm his stiffened fingers
in the flame.   The sudden red glare, glowing
through the drizzle, caught the eye of a middle-
aged man who was crossing the avenue.   So in-
secure was his footing that this momentary re-
laxation of his attention was sufficient cause for
a false step.   His feet slipped from under him
and he fell flat on his back, striking just below
the right shoulder-blade upon a compact mass
of snow, hardened by the chilly breeze, and yet
softer than the stone pavement.

The concussion knocked the breath out of
him; and he lay there for a minute almost,
gasping again and again, wholly unable to raise
himself.   As he struggled to get to his feet and
to refill his lungs with air, he heard a shop-girl

cry. "Oh, Liz, did you see him fall? Wasn't it awful?" And then he heard her companion respond. "I say. Mame, you ask him if he's hurt bad." Then two men stepped from the sidewalk and lifted him to his feet. while a boy picked up his hat and handed it to him.

"That's all right," said one of the men; "there ain't no bones broke, is there?"

The man who had fallen was getting his breath back slowly. "No," he panted. "there's nothing broke"—and he cautiously moved his limbs to make sure.

"Ye've knocked the wind out of ye." the other man returned. "but ye'll get it again in a jiffy. Come into Pat M'Cann's here and have a drink : that 'll put the life into ye again."

"That's it." agreed the man who had been helped to his feet—"that's it; get me into Pat M'Cann's—they know me there—I can rest a bit —then I'll be all right again in a little." He broke his sentences short, but even thus he was able to speak only with effort.

Taking him each by one arm. the two men helped him into the saloon almost at the door of which he had slipped. They led him straight up to the bar.

"Good-evenin'. Mr. Malone." was the barkeeper's greeting. "The boss was after askin' for ye." Then seeing the ashen face of the newcomer. he added. "It's not well ye're lookin'. What can I give ye?"

The man addressed as Malone was plainly at-
tired; his clothes were tidy but shiny; his overcoat was thin, and it was now thickly stained
down the back by the slush into which he had
fallen. The bronze button of the Grand Army
was in the buttonhole of his threadbare coat.

He steadied himself by the railing before the
bar. "Ye may give me—a little whiskey, Tom,"
he said, still gasping, "and ask these gentlemen
—what they'll take."

These gentlemen joined him in taking whiskey. Then they again assured him he would be
all right in a jiffy; and with that they left him
standing before the bar, and went their several
ways.

There was nobody else in the saloon, for the
moment, as it chanced; and Tom, the barkeeper, was able to give undivided attention to Mr.
Malone.

"It's sorry the boss 'll be to hear of yer fallin'
here at his door, an' he not there to pick ye up,"
he remarked. "But ye'd better bide till he
comes in again. Ye'll not get your breath back
so easy either—I've been knocked out myself,
an' I know—though it wa'n't no ice that downed
me."

"So Pat M'Cann wanted to see me, did he?"
asked Malone, trying to draw a long breath and
finding it impossible, as the bruised muscles of
his back refused to yield. "Oh—well, then I'll
sit me down here and wait."

"There's yer old place in the corner," Tom responded.

"I'll smoke a pipe," said Malone, moving away, "if I haven't broke it in my fall. No: I've got it right enough," he added, taking the brier-wood from the breast-pocket of his coat.

As Malone was shuffling slowly forward towards a table in a corner of the saloon, the street-door was pushed open and the owner of the bar-room entered—a tall man, with a high hat and a fur-trimmed overcoat. M'Cann went straight to the bar.

"Tom," he asked, "how many of those labor-tickets have I now in the glass there?"

Tom looked in a tumbler on the top shelf of a rack against the wall behind him. "There's five of 'em left," he answered.

"Barry M'Cormack will be in before we close and he'll ask ye for them, and ye'll give him three of them," said the owner of the saloon. "Tell him it's all I have. An' if Jerry O'Connor is here again wantin' me to go bail for his brother in the Tombs, ye must stand him off. I don't want to do it, ye see, an' I don't want neither to tell him I don't want to."

"An' what will I tell him, then?" asked the barkeeper. "Hadn't I better say ye've gone to Washington to see the Sinator?"

"Tell him what you please," responded M'Cann, "but be easy with him."

"I'll do what I can," Tom promised. "Ye

was askin' for Danny Malone before ye went out. That's him now in the corner. It's a bad fall he had out there on the ice. The drop knocked him out—but there's no bones broken."

"What I've got to tell him won't make him feel easier," returned M'Cann. "But I'll get it over as soon as I can." And with that he crossed the saloon to the farther corner, where Malone had taken his seat before a little table.

Looking up as M'Cann came towards him, Malone recognized the owner of the saloon and tried to rise to his feet; but the suddenness of his movement was swiftly resented by the strained muscles of his back, and he dropped sharply on the seat, his face wincing with the pain, which also took his breath away again.

"Well, Dan, old man," said M'Cann, "so ye've had a bad fall, sure. I'm sorry for that. Don't get up!—rest yerself there, and brace up."

The tall frame of the saloon-keeper towered stiffly beside the bent figure of the man who had had the fall, and who now looked up in the face of the other in the hope of seeing good news written there.

"Well, Pat," he began, getting his breath again. "I've had a fall—but it's nothin'—I'll be over it—in an hour or two. I'm strong enough yet—for any place ye can get me—"

He had fixed his gaze hungrily on the eyes of the other, and he was waiting eagerly for a word of hope.

The saloon-keeper lowered his glance and then cleared his throat. He had unbuttoned his overcoat and the large diamond in his shirt-front was now exposed.

Before he made answer to this appeal the elder man spoke again, overmastered by anxiety.

"Did ye see him?" he asked.

"Yes," was the response, "I saw him."

"An' will he do it for ye?" was the next passing question.

"He'd do it for me if he could, but he can't," returned M'Cann.

"He can't?" asked Malone. "An' why not?"

"Because the appointment isn't his, he says," the saloon-keeper explained. "He'd be glad to give the place to a friend of mine if he could, he told me—but there's the civil-service. He's got to follow that, he says, more by token that they raised such a row the last time he tried to beat the law."

"But I'm a veteran," pleaded the other, "I served my three years. The civil-service has got to count that, hasn't it?"

"Ye might be on the list this very minute, and it wouldn't do any good," the saloon-keeper responded; "there's veterans to burn on the list now!"

"My post will recommend me, if I ask 'em—won't that help?"

"Nothing will help, he says," M'Cann explained. "It isn't a pull that 'll do ye any good, or I could get ye the job myself, couldn't I ?"

"There ain't no influence that 'll help me, then ?" was the elder man's next question.

"As I'm tellin' ye, I done what I could, and I don't believe any man in the district couldn't do more," the saloon-keeper answered. "He says he'd rather give ye the job than not, but he can't. He's got to take the civil-service man."

"Then there ain't nothin' else you can do ?" asked Malone, hopelessly.

"I'd do anythin' I could," M'Cann replied. "But I don't see nothin' more to be done. That dog won't fight, that's all. The jig's up, there ain't no two ways about it. Of course, if I hear of anythin' else I'll tell ye—and I'll get it for ye, if I can. But it's been a pretty cold winter for the boys, so far; you know that well enough."

The other said nothing ; his head had fallen, and his eyes were staring vacantly at a box of sand across the saloon.

The saloon-keeper drew a breath of relief that the interview was over.

"Well," he said, turning away, "I must be goin' now. I've got to see the new man who's got that contract for fillin' in up on the Harlem."

"Don't think I ain't beholden to you, Pat," Malone declared, raising his head again. "Ye know I am that, and I know ye've done yer best for me."

"I did that," M'Cann admitted, taking the hand the other held out; "an' it's better I hope I can do some other time, maybe."

With that he shook Malone's hand gently and left the saloon, calling to the barkeeper as he passed, "I'll be back in an hour, if there's anybody wants me. An' make Danny Malone as comfortable as ye can. It's a bad shock he's had."

As the owner of the saloon left it three customers came in, and were served, and tossed off their drinks standing, and went out again; and the dank night-air was blown in as they swung open the outer door.

Then the barkeeper went down to the corner where Malone was sitting, with his pipe in his fingers, unlighted and unfilled, gazing fixedly at vacancy.

"Mr. Malone," he said, "is it better ye're feelin' now? Have ye got yer breath again?"

"Yes, yes," answered Malone, rousing himself, "I'm better now." And he tried to rise again; and again he sat down suddenly, seized with muscular pangs. "I'm better—but I'd best —stay here a while yet—I'm thinking."

"That's it," responded Tom, cheerfully, "get a rest here. Let me fill yer pipe for ye. There ain't nothin' so soothin' as a pipe, I don't think. An' I don't believe a drop of old ale would hurt ye, would it now?"

Five minutes later Dan Malone had his pipe alight in his mouth and a glass of ale before him on the table.   He drank the liquid slowly, barely a mouthful at a time; and he smoked irregularly also, scarcely keeping the pipe alight.   He sat there by himself, limp on the seat, with his last hope washed out of him.

Half an hour afterwards the saloon happened again to be empty, and seeing the barkeeper at liberty, Malone asked for the loan of an inkstand and a pen, and for a sheet of paper and an envelope.   When the table had been wiped off, and these things were placed on it before him, he ordered another glass of ale, and he filled his pipe again.

After he had taken a sip or two of the ale and pulled four or five times at the pipe, he squared himself painfully to the task of writing.

First, he addressed the envelope to " Hon. Terence O'Donnell, Assembly, Albany"; then he thrust this on one side to dry, and began on the letter itself.   His handwriting was more irregular than usual; it had always been cramped and straggling, but now it was shaky also.

" FRIEND TERRY,—Ime writing you this at Pat M'Canns, and its the last letter you will ever have from me. I slipped at the corner here and I fell flat on my shoulders and I knocked all the wind out of me like I was a shut bellows. I aint got it back yet. I will never have any strength again. Ime only fifty, but I had three years in the Army of the Potomac ; and fighting and sleeping in the swamp and laying out all day and all night with a wound in your leg— thats fun you got to pay for sooner or later. Ime paying

for mine now. Ime feeling very old to-night and old
men ain't no good. If Ide been younger I doubt Mary
would have shook me for Jack. Your young yet Terry
and you got a good wife, God Bless her, and youll thrive,
for your square and a good friend. But you wont never
know what it is to have the woman you loved shake you.
That hurts and it hurts just as hard even if it is your
brother she marries. Jacks only my half brother you
know but it hurt all the same. Mary married him and
hes never forgive me for the wrong he did me then. And
Mary she sides with him. Thats natural enough I suppose—hes the father of her children—but that hurts too.
Hes been doing me dirt all this winter. I know it but I
aint never let on. Now I caught him setting the kids
against me too. And theyve been friendly, both of Marys
kids have. The one named for me is a good boy and,
Terry, if you can give him a helping hand any day do it
for my sake. Ime going to pawn my watch when I leave
here to buy a pistol with. But Ill put the ticket in the
envelope with this, and some day when your feeling flush
I wish you would take it out and give it to little Danny.
I always meant him to have it.

"I ask you now for this is the last letter I will write
you and I wont never see you again. Ime smoking the
last pipe I will ever smoke and Ive drunk half of my last
glass of beer. I shall think of you when I finish it, and
it will be drinking your health and Maggies and the baby
boy your expecting.

"Ime going to quit. Ime tired, and I aint never felt so
old as I do since I had that fall an hour ago. It knocked
more out of me than wind. I was thinking Pat M'Can
here could get me a job, but he cant for fear of the civil
service. So its time I quit for good and all. Ime going
to put up my watch and get a gun. Then Ime going up
to Jacks. Mary cant refuse me a bite. Its little enough
to give me Ime thinking and its the last time Ile ask it

too.   The kids are going out to a party—a sunday school
party it is.   He see them all once more, and He say good-
by to them.   After supper when the kids are gone I will
get out the pistol and I will put the bullet where it will
do most good.   May be Jack will be sorry when its too
late may be Mary will too.   I dont know.   If they had
treated me white first off, I woodent need to buy no gun
now.

    " Good-by now, Terry, and God Bless you all.   Its time
I was going along to Marys if I want to see the kids again.
                    " Your old friend
                                " DAN MALONE."

    When he had made an end of the letter he
had a pull or two at his pipe, and then he finished his beer.   He took up what he had written
and read it over carefully to see if he had said
all that needed to be said.   Satisfied, he folded
it and tucked it inside the envelope.   After four
or five whiffs more his pipe was smoked out.
He emptied it on the table with a sharp rap, and
methodically put it back in the breast-pocket of
his coat.

    Then he raised himself to his feet slowly and
carefully, not knowing just what bruised muscle
he might chance to stretch by an inadvertent
gesture.   He shuffled across to the bar and paid
for his drinks, and asked the barkeeper if there
was a stamp to be had.   As it happened, Tom
was able to give him one, which he stuck on the
corner of the envelope.

    " Say, Mr. Malone," asked the barkeeper, " ye
don't want no tickets for the Lady Dazzlers' Co-

terie Mask and Civic Ball, to-night, do ye? It's goin' to be the most high-toned blow-out they ever had."

"I'm not goin' to balls any more," Malone answered. "I'm too old now."

Buttoning his thin overcoat tightly across the chest, he held out his hand to Tom, to the barkeeper's great surprise.

"Good-bye," he said, "Good-bye. Maybe I won't see you again, Tom."

"Good-bye. Mr. Malone," Tom answered. "But ye'll be better in the mornin'. I'm thinkin'."

"Yes," the elder man repeated, "I'll be better in the mornin'. Yes; I'm goin' to make sure of that, to-night."

When he opened the outer door of the saloon the damp moisture suddenly filled his lungs and he choked, but he dared not cough, as the strained muscles of his side warned him.

Two doors above the saloon was a pawnbroker's office, with the three golden balls hanging over the door, and with the unredeemed pledges offered for sale in the broad window. Into this store Malone made his way, glad to get out of the dank air, if only for a moment.

In perhaps five minutes he came forth holding in his hand the envelope addressed to the Honorable Terence O'Donnell. He paused on the threshold of the pawnshop and, by the light of the gas-jets in its window, he put the pawnticket into the letter and then closed it. In the large right-hand pocket of his thin overcoat there was something that had not been there when he entered the pawnbroker's—something irregular in shape; it was the revolver he had bought with the money advanced on his watch.

He turned down the avenue again, for there was a letter-box on the lamp-post at the corner occupied by M'Cann's saloon. The store between the pawnbroker's and the barroom was an undertaker's; and Malone, walking slowly past. saw in the window a little coffin, lined with white satin.

" It 'll take a bigger one than that for me," he said. "To-night's Friday—they'll be havin' the funeral on Sunday."

At the corner he dropped the letter into the box on the lamp-post, just as there came a weird shriek from an impatient tug in the river far behind him. While he was waiting for a cable-car a lame newsboy limped up to him and proffered the evening papers with a beseeching look. Malone felt in his pocket and found only two coins, a nickel and a quarter. He gave the quarter to the newsboy. Then he lifted himself painfully on the rear platform of a cable-car, and handed the nickel to the impatient conductor. The car clanged forward again; and soon the halo about its colored lamp faded away in the murky distance.

(1895)

A Glimpse of the Under World

T was a little dinner indeed, a dinner for eight only; and it was given one evening in March, in a spacious and handsome dwelling in Madison Avenue, high up on the slope of Murray Hill. The wide dining-room was at the rear of the house, and it had a broad butler's-pantry extending into the yard behind. The large kitchen was under the dining-room; and under the butler's-pantry was a room of the same size which the servants used as a parlor. In one corner of this sitting-room for the domestics was the dumb-waiter which connected with the pantry above, and in another corner was a spiral staircase which allowed the butler to descend swiftly to the kitchen in case of emergency. There was a table near the window of this servants' parlor, with a battered student-lamp on it; and around the table were grouped three or four chairs.

A whistle sounded gently in the kitchen, and the Swedish cook walked leisurely to the speaking-tube and whistled back. Then she listened, and heard the butler say, "They're all here now; I've got the oysters on the table, and I'm a-goin' in now to announce dinner to the madam. So you get that soup ready—do you hear?"

The cook did not deign to make any direct reply, but, as she left the speaking-tube and went back to the range, she said, loud enough to be heard by the servants in the sitting-room adjoining. "As though I did not know anything! I will never have another place if a black man is butler."

In the room under the pantry a sharp, wiry boy was grinning. "They're allus havin' spats, ain't they, them two? If I was Cato I wouldn't let no Dutch cook sass me, even if I was a nigger, would you?"

"Who is this young cub, when he's at 'ome?" asked the clean-shaven, trim-looking young British valet.

"He's Tim," answered the Irish laundress.

"I'm Tim," said the boy, indignantly, "that's who I am, and I'm as good as you are, too, for all you belong to a lord! And you needn't put on no frills with me, neither, for when I'm a year or two older I can lick ye!—see?"

"Don't ye mind the boy, Mr. Parsons," the Irish girl intervened. "He's no call here at all, at all. He'd run of an errand belike in the mornin' and does be sthrivin' to make himself useful. That's why they kept him here the night."

"I've got just as good a right here as he has," the boy declared, "and he doesn't come here after you either, Maggie—you're not his steady. It's that French Elise he is sparkin'."

"An' greatly I care if he is! Sparkin', in

truth! Bad cess to yer impidence." said the pleasant-faced laundress, drawing herself up. "A man, is it? It's lashins and lavins of men I could have if I'd a mind."

Fortunately the cook called Tim at this juncture and gave him a chore to do; and so left the Irish girl and the young Englishman alone.

The valet had been standing until then with his hat and cane in his hand and his overcoat across his arm. Now he laid these things on the table and took his seat by the side of the comely Irishwoman.

"Mam'zelle," he began. "is a French girl, of course, and I never could abide a foreign lingo. Now it's a pleasure for me to hear you talk, Miss Maggie."

"Ah, do be aisy, now, Mr. Parsons." she returned, coquettishly.

"It's gospel truth." he rejoined. "I enjoy talkin' to you. You keep your eyes wide open and can always tell me what's goin' on!"

"Troth, can I?" replied the laundress. "I know which ind of the egg the chicken 'll be after chippin'—every time."

"Then tell me who's dinin' 'ere to-night." the valet asked.

Before she could answer the whistle sounded faintly again, and the cook immediately brought in the green-turtle soup in the handsome silver tureen. and sent it up on the dumb-waiter. Then she returned at once to the kitchen.

"It's not a big dinner," the Irishwoman explained. "There's only eight of them. There's us three, isn't there?—Mr. and Mrs. Van Allen and Miss Ethel. Then there's your lord—and I'll go bail it's Miss Ethel he's after now? He'll be the lucky man if he gets her, too; it's a sweet angel she is."

"She won't be so unlucky to 'ave 'im neither," the Englishman returned, "mark that! She'll be Lady Stanyhurst, won't she? And my lord is a fine figure of a man, too!"

"Sure it isn't under the skin of any man that ever stepped to be worthy the likes of Miss Ethel!" said Maggie, looking at Parsons out of the corner of her eye.

"There ain't any girl in the States 'ere that wouldn't be proud to 'ave my lord," the valet retorted. "There's lots of 'em settin' their caps for 'im now. He can 'ave 'is pick, 'e can."

"The sorra cap Miss Ethel 'll set for him or any man," the laundress declared. "The boy that wants her 'll have to court her."

"I 'ave reason to believe that the marriage is arranged," Parsons asserted. "I 'ope—" then he paused, and with an effort he went on again: "I hope that 'er father is a warm man? He's good to give the girl a plum at least. I 'ope? We couldn't throw ourselves away on a girl who 'adn't a plum, you know."

"An' what might a plum be?" asked Maggie.

"A plum," the young Englishman explained,

"is a 'undred thousand pounds—'alf a million dollars, isn't it?"

"It's a whole million Mr. Van Allen can give Miss Ethel," Maggie said, "and more, too, if he wanted to. By the same token, they do be after tellin' me he has one big building downtown somewhere — I don't know — where the tenants pay him a hundred thousand dollars a year; an' they pay it, too, regular, an' nivver an eviction from one year's end to the other."

The whistle shrilled out again, and the cook made haste to place on the dumb-waiter the dish containing the fillets of sea-bass.

A few minutes later Mlle. Elise, the French maid of Miss Van Allen, entered the servants' sitting-room, and was cordially greeted by Mr. Parsons. It appeared that the Frenchwoman had been detained in Mrs. Van Allen's room relieving the guests of their wraps.

"Zat ole maid, Miss Marlenspuyk—what devil of name it is—" said Elise, "she is a true grande dame: but that Mistress Playfair—oh! I cannot suffer her! She is—how you say — made up? stuck up?"

"It's both stuck up and med up she is." the Irish laundress declared. "She's that painted her own mother wouldn't know her. An' as for stuck up, her manners is that bad there isn't none of her girls will stay in her house the second month; they gets their bit of money and they goes. Sure my brother is coachman there, and it's seven years he's had the place."

"How can he rest zere," asked the French maid, "if she is so stuck up?"

"Ah, my brother is a steady lad, and they get on very well," Maggie returned. "He knows his place, and she knows her place, too. She never says nothin' to him, and he never says nothin' to her. An' it's a good job he has, an' he don't mean to let go of it. He keeps a still tongue in his head, Danny does; but there's months when, with his wages and with his board-wages and with what he makes on the feed, the place is worth more than a hundred dollars to him."

"It's as much as a man's place is worth sometimes to accept the commission you're entitled to," the valet remarked.

"Ah, but Danny's the boy!" the laundress responded, shrewdly. "It's too much he knows about Mrs. Playfair for him to lose the job; trust him for that! As long as he wants that place he can have it an' welcome; she won't never say nothin' to him."

"Is she a widow or is she divorced, zis Mistress Playfair?" asked the French maid.

"She's the wan an' the other," said the laundress, with a laugh. "Mr. Playfair, he took and died a week after the trial, barrin' a day."

"What's this I 'ear about your Mr. Van Allen and Mrs. Playfair?" Parsons inquired.

"Is there anything between them, do you think?"

The whistle was heard again, and the cook passed before them with a saddle of mutton; and for the moment the valet's question remained unanswered.

"Who is it they have to dinner, after all?" the laundress inquired. "There's our three and your lord and Miss Marlenspuyk and Mrs. Playfair—but that's sure only six. There was to be eight all out, I'm thinkin'. It's two more men they must have."

"I heard his lordship say that he expected to meet the Lord Bishop of Tuxedo," the Englishman remarked.

"And madame say zat ze judge would be here," said the French maid.

"Judge Gillespie?" asked the valet, with a certain interest.

"Yes," the Frenchwoman answered, "the Judge Gillespie. What does that make to you zat you jump like zat?"

"Oh, nothin', nothin' at all," returned Parsons, settling himself back in his chair with a snigger.

"Out with it!" cried the Irish girl. "Don't be grinnin' all night there like a stuck pig! Out with it—I see it's on the end of your tongue."

"But yes—but yes," urged the maid, "what is it you have to laugh?"

" Really," the valet began, " I don't know that
I ought to say anything 'ere in this 'ouse, you
know — house, I mean. But I 'ave been told
that this 'ere Judge Gillespie is a very great
friend of Mrs. Van Allen's. Mind, I don't say
there's anything wrong in it, you know. I only
tell you what I 'ave 'eard tell myself in society
'ere and there. You see this ain't the only 'ouse
I visit in New York, not by a long shot it ain't.
And knowin' I visit 'ere, why, naturally, you see,
my other friends tell me the news, you know —
the news about the goin's on 'ere, you know."

The Irish laundress and the French maid
looked at each other for a moment, and then
both laughed.

" It's not outside they get the first news, is
it ?" the laundress inquired.

Apparently the maid was also going to make a
remark, but she changed her mind as the cook
again came to the dumb-waiter with the dish of
little silver saucepans containing terrapin.

The valet was somewhat puzzled by the failure
of his two attempts to open the family cupboard
of the host and hostess for an inspection of the
skeletons it might contain.

" I don't know how she has them seated at the
table." Maggie declared.

" Of course, his lordship took her in," the
Englishman declared. " A earl 'as precedence
of a judge or a bishop."

" I'd like to have a look at that lordship of

yours," the Irishwoman said, as she rose to her feet. "I'll slip up the stairs there, and maybe I can get a glimpse of 'em through the door an' no one a ha'p'orth the wiser. Is it a young man your lordship is?"

"His lordship is a young man yet," the valet replied.

"I know what that means," the laundress answered. "If he's a young man yet, I'll go bail he hasn't a hair between him an' heaven. An' to think that our Miss Ethel here is to take up with a poor hairless cratur like that. Well, well, there's no accountin' for tastes! Maybe I'll marry a Dutchman myself one of these days."

And with that she began to climb the spiral staircase in the corner of the room.

"What sort of a man is he, your milord?" asked the Frenchwoman.

"He is not a bad sort at all," the Englishman answered. "Your young lady might do worse than 'ave 'im, you know—have him, I mean. I won't say but that 'e's been a bit fast in 'is time, you know; but that's nothin' to her now, is it? 'E's sowed his wild oats long ago, and 'e's ready to marry now and settle down."

"He is zen—*défraîchi*—how you say—worn? your milord?" the Frenchwoman went on. "And mademoiselle is an angel of candor. Zey would give her *le bon Dieu* wizout confession."

"Angel or no angel," returned Mr. Parsons, "there isn't any better catch in the three king-

doms than 'is lordship to-day. 'E's a earl, isn't
'e ? And then there's the castle ! Your young
lady wouldn't be in a 'urry to let 'im go if she'd
only seen the castle, now !"

"Mademoiselle has seen ze castle," was the
answer.

" Well, I'll be damned !" said the valet.

" But yes," the French maid explained. "Last
summer, in London, your milord was presented to
mademoiselle, and he began to make his court.
Fifteen days after, when we were at Leamington,
mademoiselle and I, we go see your castle."

" It's a tip-topper now, ain't it ?" he asked.
" There's sometimes twenty and thirty of us in
the servants' 'all, and there's goin's on, and larks,
and all manner of sport. If this match comes
off, now, between 'is lordship and your young
lady, will you come with her or stay here with
her mother ?"

" Never of the life do I quit mademoiselle,"
the Frenchwoman responded.

" Then I'll 'ope to 'ave the honor of introducin'
you into the best society at the castle whenever
you come over," urged Mr. Parsons.

The Irish laundress now began to descend the
spiral stairs. The cook also came into the room
and went towards the dumb-waiter, carrying a
silver platter, on which shook and shone a dozen
little jellied cones.

" An' what might that be in thrimbles like
that ?" asked the Irishwoman, with curiosity.

" *Pâté de foie gras en aspic*," the cook responded, curtly, sending up the dish and then returning silently to the kitchen.

" Patti's photograph?" repeated the laundress.
" Do ye mind the impidence of her, tellin' me a
lie like that?"

The English valet looked at the French maid
and laughed. Then he explained, patronizingly:

" Patty de four grass, as we call it in French—
not Patti's photograph. It's a delicacy, and it's
made of goose livers."

" Then why couldn't that Dutch cook have
said so?" the laundress asked, indignantly.
" I've as good a right to know about a goose as
ever she has. I misdoubt she was that poor
where she came from they had never the grass
of a goose to their cabin."

" Did you see 'is lordship?" asked the valet.

" I did that," the Irish girl replied, " an' what
did I tell you about him? His head has grown
through his hair! There's been good and bad
harvests since he was young, I'm thinkin'—and
it's mighty quare he looks about his eyes, too.
It'll be a poor day for Miss Ethel when she marries a bald-headed ould runt like that, for all he's
a lord!"

" Oh, I say, Miss Maggie; you must not speak
so disrespectful of his lordship," Parsons insisted; " really, now, you mustn't."

" It's that Mrs. Playfair 'ud be the match for
him, I'm thinkin'," said Maggie. " It's a bold-

faced creature she is, an' no more clothes on her than ain't decent anyway. And then, how she looked at Mr. Van Allen and then at the bishop; and how she talked—I'd no patience with her. Do ye mind what it was I heard her say now?"

"How could we know what you 'eard her say?" the valet responded, impatiently.

"Sure, amn't I tellin' ye?" the Irish girl returned. "She was talkin' to the bishop, and she says, says she. 'The judge is a better man than you, bishop.' she says, 'leastwise he makes more people happy,' she says. 'How so?' says the bishop, says he. 'This way,' she says; 'when you marry a couple you make two people happy,' she says, 'an' when the judge divorces a couple he makes four people happy,' she says. Miss Ethel and the old lady with the white hair, they said nothin', but the rest of them laughed."

What further fragments of the conversation at the dinner-table up-stairs Maggie had been able to gather during her brief visit to the butler's-pantry could not then be made known to the other domestics, for Tim came slouching into the sitting-room.

"Say, Maggie," he began. "didn't you hear that ring at the bell? That's your feller—I seen him. He's out at the gate now."

"Is it the letter-man you mean?" asked Maggie, adjusting her hair as she passed the looking-glass.

"Ah, go on." returned Tim, impatiently,

"what t'ell are you givin' us? How many fellers do you want, say?"

After Maggie had chased Tim out of the room, the Swedish cook went to the dumb-waiter once more to send up the four smoking canvas-backs that lay luxuriously on their cushions of fried hominy.

The French maid and the English valet continued to chat, discussing chiefly the personal peculiarities of the members of the households in which they had served. His former masters Parsons was willing enough to find fault with, but Lord Stanyhurst he seemed to think it a point of honor to defend. Mrs. Van Allen the Frenchwoman had no high opinion of, nor of Mr. Kortright Van Allen; but of their daughter, Miss Ethel Van Allen, she could not say too much in praise.

"I told that wild Irish girl that the marriage was arranged," said Parsons, "and I'm sure I 'ope so with all my heart, for 'is lordship needs money badly—I don't mind tellin' you, mam'zelle, 'e 'asn't paid me my wages this six months, not that I'd demean myself by askin' for them. But is it really settled, after all?—that's what I'd like to know."

"I zink so," the Frenchwoman responded; "you see, mademoiselle is not happy here. Monsieur and madame are at drawn knives. Zey have not spoken since two years."

"Mr. and Mrs. Van Allen don't speak to each

other?" asked Parsons, with great interest. "But they must be speaking to each other there at dinner now."

"Oh, at dinner, yes," the French maid explained; "in the world, yes, zey talk zemselves. But at ze house, never a word. Zat is so sad for mademoiselle, is it not? It is not remarkable zat she marry herself with anybody to get out of ze house."

"Oh, ho!" rejoined the valet. "I see, I see! But if that's the way she's been brought up, you know, I don't believe she will 'it it off with 'is lordship."

"If he makes her not happy, your milord—" began the maid, forcibly, "but he must. He must render her happy, for she will have nobody to go to after ze marriage except her husband."

"Whatever do you mean by that?" asked Parsons, a little suspiciously.

"I know what I mean," she responded. "Monsieur and madame only attend till mademoiselle is married, and zen zey are divorced. Zey don't tell me zat, no—but I know."

"Yes," the valet admitted, "it ain't so very 'ard to find out a thing like that."

"And I know more yet," added the French maid. "I am not blind, am I? I can see that two and two make four, is it not? Zen, I tell you zat after ze marriage of mademoiselle, monsieur and madame are divorced, zat is one zing. Zen madame will marry zat Judge Gil-

lespie, and monsieur will marry zat Madame
Playfair—you see!"

"That would be a rum start, now, wouldn't
it?" was the only comment of Parsons.

At this moment the portly form of Cato, the
black butler, was seen descending the staircase
in the corner of the room.

As soon as the aged negro's white head was
visible he paused, and leaning over the light
iron railing he addressed himself to the young
Englishman.

"Misto' Parsons," he said, solemnly. "yo' lord
knows a good thing when he gets it, sah! He
tasted my celery salad, and he said to Mrs. Van
Allen that he hadn't never eaten no better salad
than that, sah, and I don't believe he never did,
neither!"

So saying he slowly withdrew up-stairs again,
as the cook advanced to the dumb-waiter carrying the Nesselrode pudding.

(1896)

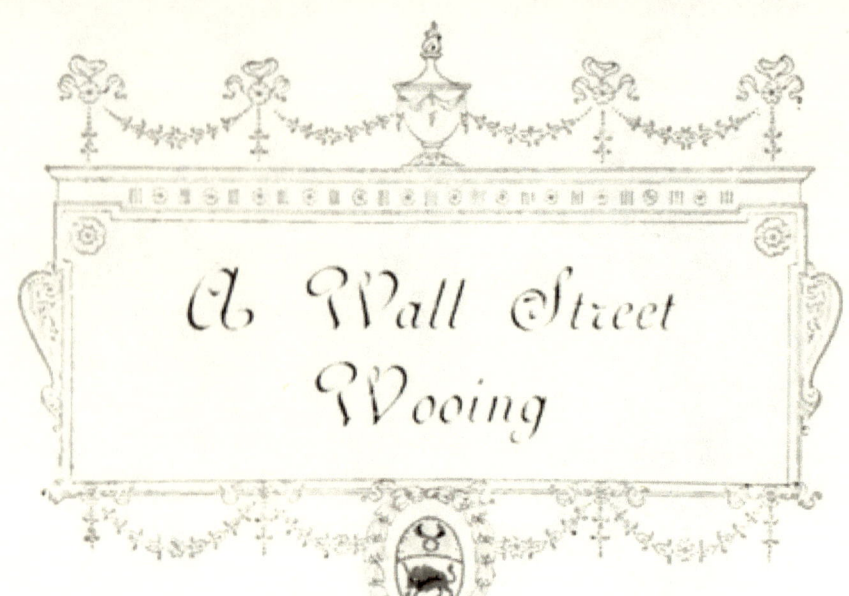

A Wall Street Wooing

T had poured all the night before, and even now, at three o'clock in the afternoon, the air had the washed clearness that follows a warm rain. Fortunately the sun had shone forth before the church bells summoned the worshippers to kneel in front of the marble altars, banked high with scentless white flowers. It was Easter, and the first of April also; and, furthermore, the first warm Sunday of the spring. So the young men and maidens who clustered about the doors of the churches that afternoon were decked out in fresh apparel—the young men in light overcoats, and the maidens in all the bravery of their new bonnets.

In the corner of one of the cable-cars which were sliding along under the skeleton of the elevated railroad there sat a young man looking at his neighbors with begrudging interest, and pulling at the ends of an aggressive black mustache. Filson Shelby was not yet at home in the great city, and he knew it, and he silently protested against it. He was forever on the watch for a chance to resent the complacent attitude of city folks towards country people. Yet the metropolis had so far conquered him

that his hat and his shoes and his clothes were
city made.

It was six months now since the young Southwesterner had left his native village, and already
he thought that he knew New York pretty well,
from Harlem where he boarded to Wall Street
where he worked. He was sure that he was well
informed as to the customs of New-Yorkers, although the New-Yorkers changed their customs
so rapidly that it was not so easy to be certain
about this.

There were white flowers blossoming in the
parlor windows of many of the houses in Fifty-
third Street, through which the cable-car was
passing, and as the car clanged around the curve
and started on its way down Seventh Avenue it
grazed the tail of a florist's wagon, the box of
which was piled high with palms. Filson Shelby
was aware that it was now a practice of New-Yorkers to give one another potted plants at Easter.

He had been told also that the habit no longer
obtained of paying calls on Sunday afternoon;
and none the less was he on his way down to
Wall Street to take out for a walk the one girl
in New York who seemed to him to have the un-
pretending simplicity of the girls of the South-
west. What did he care, he asked himself, whether or not it was fashionable to call on girls Sunday
afternoon? What right had the New-Yorkers,
anyhow, to assume that their way of doing things
was the only right and proper way?

Having propounded these questions to himself, he answered them with a smile, for he had a saving sense of humor, and even a tendency towards self-analysis, and he had long ago detected his own pride in living in New York. In his earliest letters home he had expressed his delight in that he was now at the headquarters of the whole country; and he had written these letters on broad sheets of paper bought in the German quarter, and adorned with outline views of the sights of the city, picked out in the primary colors. He had sent missives thus decorated not only to his family and to his old friends, but even to mere acquaintances of his boyhood, for whom he cared little or nothing, except that they should know him to be settled in the metropolis. He could not but suspect that if he were now to go back to the village of his birth, he would seem as stuck-up to the natives as the New-Yorkers had seemed to him the first few weeks he was in the city.

The car slipped down Seventh Avenue, and stumbled into Broadway, and sped along sometimes with a smooth swiftness and again with a jerky hesitation. Gayly dressed family groups got on and got off, and the car had almost emptied itself by the time it came to Madison Square. Filson Shelby was greatly interested in the manners of two handsomely gowned girls who sat opposite to him, and who did not know each other very well. It struck him that one of them

—the prettier of the two, as it happened—was
a little uneasy in the other's company, and yet
pleased to be seen with her. To his regret, both
of them alighted at Grace Church, leaving only
half a dozen people in the long car as it started
again on its journey down-town.

He set down the plainer of the two as a member of the strange society known as the "Four
Hundred," about which he had heard so much
since he had been reading the Sunday papers.
If he were right in this ascription, and if he
were to judge by this sample, the girls of the
Four Hundred were not a very good-looking lot,
for all they were so stylishly dressed. It struck
him, too, that this girl's manners were somehow
offensive, although he could not state precisely
where the offence lay.

He was glad that the one girl in New York
whom he knew at all well had the easy good manners which spring from a naturally good heart.
She was as well educated as the two girls who
had just left the car; perhaps better, for she was
going to graduate from the Normal College in
two or three months; and yet she was unaffected
and unassuming. As he phrased it in his mind,
"she didn't put on any frills." He could chat
with her just as easily as he used to talk to the
girls who had gone to school with him at home.
And yet when he considered how unlike she was
really to these friends of his childhood he wondered why it was he and she had got along so

well, and his thoughts went back to the occasion
of his first meeting with her.

The car was now speeding swiftly down Broadway, obstructed by no carriages, no carts, no
trucks, no wagons, and no drays.   Below Astor
Place the sidewalks were as bare as the street itself was empty.   The shades were down in the
windows of the many-storied buildings which
towered above the deserted thoroughfare, and
the flamboyant signs made their incessant ap-
peals in vain.   For a mile or more it was almost
as though he were being carried through the
avenues of an abandoned city.   The one evidence
of life, other than the cars themselves, was an
infrequent bicyclist " riding the cable slot " up
from the South Ferry.   If only he had first arrived in New York in the restful quiet of a Sunday, so the young Southwesterner found himself
thinking, perhaps the metropolis might not have
seemed to him so overwhelming.   As it was, it
had been a shock to him to be plunged suddenly
into the vortex of the immense city.

A telegrapher in the little town near which
he was born, Filson Shelby had gone beyond his
duty to oblige a New-Yorker who had chanced
to be detained there for a fortnight, and the
New-Yorker had repaid his courtesy by the
proffer of a position as private operator in the
office of a Wall Street friend.   The young man
had accepted eagerly, having no ties to bind him
to his home; and yet he had felt desperately

homesick more than once during his first three
months in New York. Indeed, it was not until
he had come to know Edna Leisler that he had
reconciled himself to the great town, which was
so crowded, and in which he was so alone. He
was slow to form friendships, but he had made
a few acquaintances.

It was one of these casual acquaintances who
had taken him one day to the top of an old office
building not far from the Stock Exchange. Here
the janitor lived, and was allowed to use one of
the rooms allotted to him as a lunch-room. The
janitor's wife was a good cook, and Filson Shelby
returned there again and again. One Saturday,
when the room happened to be more crowded
than usual, the rawboned and ruddy Irish girl
was unable to serve everybody, and some time
after he had given his order Filson Shelby was
waited upon by a young lady in a neat brown
dress. He was observant, and he saw a red spot
burning on each cheek, and he noted that the
lips were tightly set. It seemed to him that she
was acting as waitress unwillingly, and yet at
the same time that she was doing it of her own
accord. He did not like to stare at her, and yet
he could hardly take his eyes from her while she
was in the room. She was not beautiful exactly,
for she was but a slim slip of a girl, and she had
coppery hair; and he had always been taught
that red hair was ugly. Yet something about
her took his fancy; perhaps it was her inde-

pendent manner. perhaps it was rather her perky
self-possession : perhaps. after all. it was the humorous expression which lurked in her eyes and
at the corner of her mouth.

He had lingered over his luncheon that noon
as long as he could. and then he was reward-
ed. The man who had first brought him there
entered and took a seat beside him. When the
young lady in brown came for his order the new-
comer shook hands with her cordially, and called
her "Miss Edna."

"She used to go to school with my sister," he
explained to the young Southwesterner. "She's
up at the Normal College now. and I've never
seen her here in the dining-room before. But
she has a holiday, and I suppose she thought she
ought to help her mother out. It's her mother
who cooks, you know—and boss cooking it is.
too. isn't it ?—real home sort of flavor about it."

Filson Shelby had still delayed his departure :
and as Edna Leisler brought bread and butter.
and went back again to the kitchen. his friend's
chatter had streamed along.

"Red-hot hair, hasn't she ?" was the next
remark. "If there was half a dozen more of
her you'd think it was a torchlight procession,
wouldn't you ? But it suits her style. don't it ?
Fact is. she's the only red-haired girl I ever saw
I didn't hate at sight."

It seemed as though he had expected Filson
to respond to this, and so the young Southwest-

erner hesitated, and cleared his throat, and admitted that her hair was red.

" Well, it *is* just," the other returned. " I guess her barber has to wear asbestos gloves, eh ? But she's a good girl, Edna is, if she is a brand from the burning. My sister used to be very fond of her, and I like her myself, though she isn't in our set exactly. I'll introduce you, if you like ?"

The cable-car now came to a halt sharply to set down passengers for Brooklyn by way of the bridge, but Filson Shelby was wholly unconscious of this. He was busy with the recollection of that winter day when he had stood up with bashful awkwardness and had heard Edna Leisler say that she was pleased to meet him. He had the memory also of the next Saturday, when he had gone back to the little low eating-room under the roof in the hope of seeing her again, and of the unaffected frankness of her manner towards him when he met her on the stairway.

He remembered how simply she had accepted his invitation to go to Central Park to lunch on Washington's Birthday, the first holiday when they were both free, and he remembered, too, what a good time they had up there. It was on that Washington's Birthday that he had first found out that in the eyes of some people red hair was not a blemish, but a beauty. The omnibus in which they came down-town had been so crowded that they were separated, and he heard one well-dressed man say to his companion: "Did you ever see such stunning hair as that girl has? It is like burnished copper—except when the sun glints on it, and then it's like spun gold."

Hitherto he had been willing to overlook her aggressive locks in consideration of her good qualities, but thereafter he came rapidly to accept the view of the well-dressed man in the omnibus, and to look upon her red hair as a crown of glory. She did not seem any more attractive to him than she did at first meeting, but he knew now that other men might be attracted also. He wondered whether there were any other men whom she knew as well as she knew him. It seemed to him that they had taken to each other at the start, and they were now very good friends indeed. But there was no reason why she should not have other friends also.

The current of his retrospection was not so sweeping that he could not follow the course of the cable-car in which he was seated, and just then he saw the brown spire of Trinity Church and heard the clock strike three. He signalled to the conductor, and the car stopped before the church door and at the head of Wall Street.

As he stood looking down the crooked street, washed white by the rain and looking clean in the April sunshine, he asked himself why he was going to meet Edna Leisler—and especially why it was his heart had slowed up at the suggestion that perhaps other men were as attentive to her as he was. He was not in love with her, was he? That she had made New York tolerable to him he was ready to admit, and also that he liked her better than any girl he had ever met. But if he was jealous of her, did not that prove that he loved her?

These were the questions he propounded as he walked from Broadway to the old building on the top floor of which the Leislers lived. When Edna Leisler came down-stairs to meet him, with her new Easter hat, he knew the answers to these questions; he knew that he would be miserable if he were to lose the privilege of her society; he knew furthermore that he had loved her since the first day he had seen her, even though he had not hitherto suspected it. He knew also that he would never have a better chance to tell her that he loved her than he would have that afternoon; and while they were shaking hands he made up his mind that before he took her back to her mother's he would get her promise to marry him.

With this resolve fixed, he took refuge in the commonplace.

"Am I late?" he asked.

"Five minutes," she answered. "I didn't know but what you were going to April-fool me."

"Oh, Miss Edna," he cried, "you know I wouldn't do that!"

"I didn't think you would really," she laughed
back. "And I felt sure I could get even with
you if you did."

Thus lightly chatting, they came to the corner
of Broad Street.

"Shall we go down to the Battery?" he suggested, thinking that he might find a chance
there to say what was in his heart.

"Yes," she assented; "it 'll be first-rate to
get a whiff of the salt breeze. It's as warm as
spring to-day, isn't it?"

In front of the Stock Exchange, and for two
or three blocks below, Broad Street was absolutely bare, except for a little knot of men working over a man-hole of the electrical conduit.
The ten-story buildings lifted themselves aloft
on both sides of the street, without any evidence
of life from window or doorway: they were as
silent and seemingly empty as though they belonged to a deserted city of the plains. Bar-
rooms in cellars had bock-beer placards before
their closed portals. On the glass panel of the
swing-door which admitted the week-day passer-
by to the Business Men's Quick Lunch there was
wafered the bill of fare of the day before, but
the door itself was closed tight. So were the en-
trances to more pretentious restaurants.

But as Filson Shelby and Edna Leisler went
on farther down-town, Broad Street slowly
changed its character. There were not so many
office buildings and more retail shops; there

were a few wholesale warehouses ; there were
even cheap flat - houses ; and there were more
signs of life. Children began to fill the road-
way and the sidewalks. There were boys on tri-
cycles, and there were Little Mothers pushing
perambulators in which babies lay asleep. There
were girls on roller-skates ; and one of these, a
tall, lanky child, had a frolicsome black poodle,
which pulled her quickly along the sidewalk.

Seeing some of these things, and not seeing
others, and being taken up wholly by their own
talk, the young Southwesterner and the New
York girl passed through Whitehall Street and
came out on the Battery. They walked to the
edge of the water, and looked across the waves
to the Statue of Liberty holding her torch aloft.
An Italian steamer full of immigrants was just
coming up from Quarantine. The afternoon was
clear, after the rain of the night before, and yet
there was a haze on the horizon. The huge
grain - elevators over on the Jersey shore stood
out against the sky defiantly.

A fringe of men and women sat on the seats
around the grass - plots and along the sea-wall.
Many of the women had children in their arms
or at their skirts. Most of the men were reading the gaudily illustrated Sunday newspapers ;
some of them were smoking. The sea - breeze
blew mildly, with a foretaste of warm weather.
The grass-plots were brownish-gray, with but the
barest touch of green at the edges, and there was

never a bud yet on any of the skeleton trees.
None the less did every one know that the winter
was gone for good, and that any day almost the
spring might come in with a rush.

As Filson Shelby looked about him he saw
more than one young couple sitting side by side
on the benches or sauntering languidly along the
winding walks, and he knew that he was not the
only young fellow who felt the stirring of the
season. No one of the other girls was as good-
looking as Edna, nor as stylish; he saw this at
half a glance. With every minute his desire
grew to tell her how dear she was to him, and
still he put it off and put it off. Once or twice
when she spoke to him he left her remark unanswered, and then hastily begged her pardon for
his rudeness. He did not quite know what he
was saying, and he feared that she must think
him a fool. He was restless, too, and it seemed
to him quite impossible to ask her to marry him
in such an exposed place as the Battery.

"Suppose we go up to Trinity Church?" he
suggested. "It's always quiet enough in the
graveyard there."

"Isn't it quiet enough here?" she asked, as
they turned their footsteps away from Castle
Garden.

"It isn't really noisy, I'll admit," he responded; "but I get mighty tired of those elevated
trains snorting along over the back of my head,
don't you?"

5

She gave him a queer little look out of the corner of her eye, and then she laughed lightly.

"Oh, well," she replied, "if you think Trinity Church Yard is a better place, I don't mind."

Then her cheeks suddenly flamed crimson, and she turned away her head.

They were now crossing the barren space under the elevated railroad, and, as it happened, the young man did not see her swift blush.

As they skirted the oval of Bowling Green the girl nodded to a gray-coated policeman on guard over the little park.

"Who's that?" asked the young man, acutely jealous, although he saw that the officer was not less than fifty years old.

"That's Mr. O'Rourke," she explained. "He's Rose O'Rourke's father. She was graduated from the Normal College only two years ago, and then she went on the stage. She's getting on splendidly, too. She played Queen Elizabeth last year —and didn't she look it? I'm sure she's a great deal handsomer than that old Queen was."

"But that old Queen," he returned, "wasn't the daughter of a sparrow-cop—that's what you call them, don't you?"

"*I* don't call them so," she responded, "for I think it's vulgar to talk slang."

"But the boys do call a park policeman a sparrow-cop, don't they?" he persisted.

"The little boys do," she answered, "but I know Mr. O'Rourke doesn't like it."

"I can understand that," he replied. "If I had Queen Elizabeth for a daughter, I think I should want to be a king myself."

"Well," the girl went on to explain. "Rose did want him to give up his appointment. She said she was earning enough for her father not to work. But he wouldn't, for all she urged him. She's a kind girl, is Rose, and not a bit stuck-up. She came up to the college last year and recited for us. You should have heard her do 'Curfew shall not ring to-night'; I tell you she was splendid."

"I don't believe she did it any better than you could," he declared.

"Oh, don't you?" she returned, heartily; "that's only because you didn't hear her. And she was very nice to me, too. She complimented me on my piece."

"What did you speak?" he asked.

"Oh, I always choose something fiery and patriotic. I spoke 'Sheridan's Ride' first, and then, when the girls encored me, I spoke 'Old Ironsides'—but I like 'Sheridan's Ride' best ; and Rose O'Rourke said I got more out of it than anybody she had ever heard. But then she always was so complimentary."

"I reckon she knows it's lucky for her you don't go on the stage," the lover asserted. "It would be a cold day for her if you did. I haven't seen her, but I'm sure she isn't such a good looker as you are !"

"Thank you for the compliment," the girl answered. "If we weren't here in Broadway, in front of Trinity Church, I'd drop you a courtesy. But you wouldn't say that if you had seen her, for she's as pretty as a picture."

"Do you mean that she is as fresh as paint?" he asked.

"That's real mean of you," she retorted, "for Rose doesn't need to paint at all, even on the stage; she has just the loveliest complexion."

"She's not the only girl in New York who has a lovely complexion," he declared; and again the color rose swiftly on her cheek, and then as swiftly faded.

They had now come to the gates of Trinity Church, and they saw a little stream of men and women pouring in to attend the afternoon service.

"You must not be down on Rose," the girl said, as they turned away from Broadway and began to ramble slowly amid the tombstones. "She's a good friend of mine. She said she'd get me an engagement if I'd go on the stage—"

"But you are not going to?" he broke in, earnestly.

"I'd love to," she answered, calmly. "But I'm too big a coward. I'd never dare stand up before the people in a great big theatre and feel they were all looking at me."

"I'm glad you're not going to," he declared. "It would be too delightful for anything!"

she asserted ; "but I'd never have the courage. I know I wouldn't, so I've given up the idea. I'll finish my course at the college, and get my diploma, and then I'll be a teacher—that is, if I can get an appointment. But it isn't easy if you haven't any influence ; and father doesn't take any interest in politics, and he doesn't know any of the trustees of this district, and I can't see how I'm ever to get into a school. Now Mr. O'Rourke could help me if he wanted—"

"The sparrow-cop ?" interrupted the young Southwesterner. "Why, what has he got to do with the public schools ?"

"Mr. O'Rourke has a great deal of influence in this ward, I can tell you that." she returned. "He has a pull on more than one of the trustees. If he were to back me, I'd get my position sure ! And maybe I had better go to Rose and ask her for her father's influence."

They were now almost in the centre of that part of the church-yard which lies above the church, and behind the monument to the American prisoners who died during the British occupancy of New York. The afternoon service was about to begin, and the solemn tones of the organ were audible where they stood.

It seemed to Filson Shelby that the time had come for him to speak.

He swallowed a lump in his throat, and began.

"Miss Edna," he said, hesitatingly, "why do you want to be a school-teacher?"

"To earn my living, to be sure!" she answered, calmly enough, although the color was rising again on her cheeks.

"But you don't need ever so many scholars to earn your living, do you?" he asked, gaining courage slowly.

"What do you mean?" she returned, forcing herself to look him in the face.

"I mean," he responded, "that I don't see why you couldn't earn your living just as well by having only one scholar—"

"Only one scholar?" she echoed.

"Yes—only one scholar," he declared; "but you could take him for life. And you could teach him everything that was good and true and beautiful—and he would work hard for you, and try and make you happy."

The color ebbed from her cheeks, but she said nothing. The low notes of the organ were dying away, and on the elevated railroad just behind the young couple a train came hissing along wreathed in swirling steam.

"I'm not worthy of you, Edna; I know that only too well; but you can make me ever so much better if you'll only try," he urged. "I love you with my whole heart—that's what I've been trying to say. Will you marry me?"

She raised her eyes to his and simply answered, "Yes."

IN TRINITY CHURCH-YARD

An hour later, as they were going through the dropping twilight down Wall Street to the old office building, on the top floor of which she lived with her parents, they were still talking of each other, of their united future, and of their separate past.

When they came to the door and stood at the foot of the five flights of stairs that led up to the janitor's apartment, they had still many things to say to each other.

What seemed to Filson Shelby most astonishing was that he should now be engaged to be married, when that very morning he was not even aware of his love for her. And being a very young fellow, and, moreover, being very much in love, he could not keep this astonishing thing to himself, but must needs tell her.

"Do you know, Edna," he began, "that I must have been in love with you a long while without knowing it? Isn't that most extraordinary? And it was only this morning that I found it out!"

Standing on the stairs above him, and just out of his reach, she broke into a merry little laugh, and the tendrils of red hair quivered around her broad brow.

"What are you laughing at?" he asked.

"Oh, nothing," she answered, and then she laughed again. "At least, not much. It is only because men are so much slower to see things than women are."

"What do you mean?" he asked again.

"Well," she returned, laughing once more, and retreating two or three steps higher up the stairs, "I mean that you say you only found out this morning that you were in love with me—"

"Yes?"

"Well," she continued, making ready for flight, "I found it out more than two months ago."

(1895)

A Spring Flood in Broadway

S he came down the steps of his sister's little house, that first Saturday in May, he saw before him the fresh greenery of the grass in Stuyvesant Square and the delicate blossoms on its sparse bushes and the young leaves on its trees : and he felt in himself also the subtle influences of the spring-tide. The sky was cloudless, serene, and unfathomably blue. The sun shone clearly, and the shadows it cast were already lengthening along the street. The gentle breeze blew hesitatingly. He heard the inarticulate shriek of the hawker bearing a tray containing a dozen square boxes of strawberries and walking near a cart piled high with crates. When he crossed Third Avenue he noticed that a white umbrella had flowered out over the raised chair of the Italian boot-black at the corner. A butcher-boy, with basket on arm, was lingering at a basement door in lively banter with a good-looking Irish cook. A country wagon, full of growing plants, crawled down the street while the vender bawled forth the cheapness of his wares.

There were other signs of the season at Union Square—the dingy landaus with their tops half open, the flowers bedded out in bright profusion, the aquatic plants adorning the broad basin of the fountain, the pigeons wooing and cooing languidly, the sparrows energetically flirting and fighting, the young men and maidens walking slowly along the curving paths and smiling in each other's faces. To Harry Grant, just home from a long winter in the bleak Northwest, it seemed as though man and nature were alike rejoicing in the rising of the sap and the bourgeoning of spring. It was as though the pulse of the strong city were beating more swiftly and with renewed youth. Harry Grant felt his own heart rejoice that he was back again amid the sights he loved, within a stone's-throw of the house where he was born, within pistol-shot of the residence of the girl he was now going at last to ask to marry him.

It was nearly a year since he had last seen her, but he knew she would greet him as cordially as she had always done. That Winifred was a good friend of his he knew well enough ; what he did not know at all was whether or not the friendship had changed to love on her part also. He could hardly recall the time when he had not known her. He could distinctly remember the occasion when he had first told her that he intended to marry her when he was grown up— that was on a spring day like this, and he was seven and she was five, and they were playing together in Gramercy Park while their nurses fol-

lowed them slowly around the enclosure. Now
he was twenty-three and she was twenty-one :
and in all these sixteen years there had been no
day when he had not looked forward to their
marriage. Of course, when he had grown to be
a big boy and had been sent away to boarding-
school, he had been ashamed to talk about such
things. But when he went to college he had
gazed ahead four years and almost fixed on the
day he intended to propose.

Then his father had died, and the family af-
fairs were left in inexplicable confusion. His
uncle had offered to pay Harry's way through
Columbia. but he was in a haste to be independent, to make his own path, to have a position
which he could ask Winifred to share. He found
a place at once in the office of a great dry-goods
house : and he had been so successful there that
one of their customers had offered him induce-
ments to go out to a swiftly growing city in the
new Northwest. Two years had Harry Grant
spent out there—two years of hard work amid
men who were all toiling mightily and who were
capable of appreciating his youthful energy.
Now he was back again in New York to act as
the Eastern representative of the chief capitalist
of the Northwestern city. an old man, who liked
Harry, and who saw how useful his address and
his character might be. The position was oner-
ous for a man so young : but it was honorable
also. and the salary was liberal even from a New

York standpoint. At last he was again able to look at life from the point of view of a New-Yorker. At last he was ready to ask her to share his life.

He was in no hurry for the moment, as he could not make sure of finding her at home until nearly five o'clock, and it was now barely four by the transparent dial which Atlas bore on his back in the jeweller's upper window on the opposite side of the square. He crossed Broadway at Fourteenth Street, and there he was caught up at once and swept along by the spring-flood rolling up from down-town that beautiful afternoon in May. The windows of the florists' were lovely with Easter lilies and fragrant with branches of lilac. The windows of the confectioners' were gay with gaudy Easter eggs and with elaborate chocolate rabbits. Young girls pressed giggling through the doors to stand packed beside the soda-water fountains. Elderly men lingered at the street corners to stare at the young women.

Within an hour or two at the most Harry Grant intended to ask Winifred to be his wife, and as he saw the dread question so close before him he could not but wonder what the answer would be. Winifred liked him—that much he felt sure about. Whether she loved him, even a little, that he could not venture to guess. She had sturdy common-sense and she was self-reliant, he knew well, and yet he could not help fearing that perhaps the influence of her grandmother had been more powerful than he wished. It was possible, of course, that the restless and ambitious old lady had inoculated her young granddaughter with some of her own dissatisfaction.

As Harry's circumstances had changed since they were boy and girl together, so had Winifred's. Her father had died also, and then her grandfather, leaving a very large fortune to his widow, and Winifred had gone to live with her grandmother, Mrs. Winston-Smith. (It was her grandmother who had put the hyphen into the name, and who had insisted on its adoption by the son and the granddaughter.) That Mrs. Winston-Smith did not like him, Harry Grant knew only too well, or, at least, that she did not approve of him as a possible suitor for the hand of Miss Winston-Smith. She thought that her granddaughter ought to make a brilliant marriage. She had been heard to say that in England Winifred would have no difficulty in marrying a title. She had taken her granddaughter to London the season before, and they had been presented at court, to go afterwards on a round of country-house visits, returning late to finish the summer at Lenox.

All this Harry knew from the newspapers; but what Winifred had thought of it all he did not know, for he had not seen her since the day before her departure for England. And that interview itself had been in the presence of the grandmother and of two or three casual callers. Really he had not had chance of speech with the woman he had loved for three years—ever since Mrs. Winston-Smith had asked him to dinner one night, only to take him into the library and to tell him that she saw that he was attracted by Winifred, and no wonder, but that he must give up the hope of winning her. Mrs. Winston-Smith was some sixty-years old at the time of this talk with Harry Grant, and she was a very stately dame, with no lack of manner, but she could, if she chose, express herself with absolute frankness and directness. On that occasion she had seen fit to be perfectly plain-spoken. She had told him that Winifred had been used to luxury and could not do without it, and that if Winifred married against her wishes she would give all her money to the new cathedral, cutting the girl off without a cent. She asked Harry if he did not think it would be very selfish of him to press his suit when its success would mean the misery of the woman he pretended to love. She reminded him that his own income was meagre, and that he had no prospects. If, then, Winifred had no money, how could she as his wife have all the luxuries to which she was accustomed, and which had now become necessities? Of course she did not admit that Winifred was in any way interested in him. In fact, she hoped and trusted that the girl's affections were in no way engaged; and she relied on Mr.

Grant's good sense and on his unwillingness to be so brutally selfish. After all, Winifred was a mere child, and had seen nothing of the world as yet.

Harry Grant had made no promises to Mrs. Winston-Smith, but he had felt the force of some of her arguments. Plainly he had no right to ask the woman he loved to give up everything for his sake; and as plainly he had no wish to live on any money her grandmother might give her. He meant, more than ever, to win her for his wife; but he saw clearly that he must make himself independent first. To be able to give her a home not unworthy of her he had worked hard all these years. At last he had succeeded, and he was in a position to ask her to marry him without at the same time asking her to surrender the most of the little comforts which made her life easy. With the salary he had now he could make her comfortable, even if her grandmother chose to take offence and cut her off without a cent. There was no false pride about the young fellow, and he did not pretend to himself that he did not care whether or not the grandmother carried out her threat. He was well aware that life would be very much pleasanter if Mrs. Winston-Smith should accept the situation and make the best of it, and give her granddaughter an adequate allowance.

Then, as these thoughts ran through his head, he smiled at his own fatuity in taking Winifred's

consent for granted in this summary fashion.
What Mrs. Winston-Smith said or did mattered
little.   What was of vital importance was Winifred's own answer to his question.   He could not
but recognize that to call on a young lady after
a year's separation and to ask her in marriage,
suddenly, without warning, was an unusual proceeding.   And yet that was just what he was
going to do; and he found himself musing over
schemes for getting her away from her grandmother and from any chance visitors.   He tried
to devise a means of luring her into the library
or of coaxing her into the conservatory.   He
cared not how soon they might be interrupted;
he knew what he had to say, and he was prepared
to say it briefly.   Five minutes would be time
enough — five minutes, if he could but have
them clear.   When a man has been wanting for
years to be able to put a simple question, it ought
not to take him long to say the needful words;
and he knew that Winifred would not keep him
waiting for his answer.   Whether it was to be
yes or no, she would know her own mind, and
be ready and willing to accept him at once or to
reject him with as little hesitation.

He had been keeping pace with the throng
that was sweeping massively up-town, but as the
fear seized him that, after all, he had little right
to think she might love him, he lengthened his
stride in futile impatience to get his answer
sooner.   He glanced up at Tiffany's clock, then

almost over his head, and he slackened his speed as he saw that it was not yet five minutes past four. He had at least half an hour to wait before he could hope to find her at home.

Then, most unexpectedly, he was favored with fortune. The foremost of the carriages drawn up in Fifteenth Street alongside the jeweller's was a handsome coupé, in which a young lady was sitting alone. As Harry Grant drew near to the corner his glance fell on this coupé, and at that moment the young lady looked up. He saw that it was Winifred. As their eyes met a swift blush bloomed in her face, and faded as speedily. She smiled and held out her hand and laughed happily as he sprang to the door of the carriage.

"Winifred!" he cried.

"Harry!" she answered.

"I didn't expect to see you here!" he declared.

"Is that the reason you are here, then?" she returned.

He made no reply. He could not take his eyes from her. In his delight at seeing her again he had nothing to say.

"Well?" she asked, when she thought he had stared enough.

"Well," he answered, "I couldn't help it. You are prettier than ever."

Again a flush flitted across her face, fainter this time, and fleeting sooner.

"That's a very direct compliment, don't you think?" she retorted, withdrawing her hand, which he had kept clasped in his own. "And you are looking well, too. Your life out West there is good for you. I don't wonder you prefer it to this noisy old New York of ours."

"But I don't prefer it," he declared, hotly. "A week of New York is worth a year of the whole wide West put together. And I've done with all that now. I've come back here for good now—"

"Have you really?" she responded, as he hesitated, having so much to say that he did not know where to begin.

"I got back this morning," he explained. "and I was coming to see you this afternoon. I've—I've so many things to tell you."

She looked at him for a second, and then she glanced away, as she said: "You will have to talk very fast, then, if you have so many things to tell me. We are going to sail on Tuesday morning, and this afternoon we are off to Tuxedo for over Sunday."

"You sail on Tuesday?" he cried, despairingly. "Just when I have come back on purpose to see you again!"

"You didn't telegraph grandma that you were coming, or she might have made other arrangements," the young woman retorted, with a little laugh.

"And if you are going to Tuxedo to-night,"

"'WINIFRED!' HE CRIED"

he continued. paying no heed to this ironic suggestion. "then you won't be at home this afternoon?"

"No." she answered: "we shall be back just in time to dress and get away to the train. Grandma has two or three errands to do first— she's inside there arranging about some silver things she wants to take over with us."

"But I must see you to-day," he pleaded.

"Aren't you seeing me now?" she returned. as the blush rose again and fell.

"But I've got something I want to say to you!" he urged.

"Won't it keep till Monday afternoon?" she asked, with another light laugh; but beneath the levity there was more than a hint of feeling.

"No," he declared; "it won't keep an hour longer, for it's been kept too many years already. I've come here on purpose to tell you something —and I must do it to-day!"

"If it's something you want to tell grandma—" she began, as if to gain time.

"But it isn't." he returned. leaning his head almost inside the open window of the carriage. "It's you I want to talk to—not to your grandmother."

"Then," said she, with a subtle change of manner, "if it is something you don't want grandma to hear, don't try to say it now. for here she comes."

Harry Grant gave a hasty glance behind him,

and he recognized the stately figure of Mrs. Winston-Smith in conversation with one of the salesmen just inside the door of the great store.

"Winifred," he said, pleadingly, taking her hand again, "where can I see you again, if only for a minute—only a minute? That's enough for what I want!"

Winifred looked at him and then down at her fingers. She hesitated, and finally she answered:

"I think I heard grandma say she was going to the florist's before she went home—that florist in Broadway near Daly's, you know. She has a lot of things to order there, and I shall sit in the carriage."

"I'll take the cable-car and be there waiting for you," he responded.

"Don't let grandma see you," she cried; "that is—well—"

Then she sank back on the cushions of the carriage, for Mrs. Winston-Smith was about to leave the store.

Harry Grant had caught sight of the old lady in time. He stepped away from the carriage, and, passing behind it, crossed to the other side of the street without giving Winifred's grandmother a chance to recognize him.

He waited on the opposite corner until Mrs. Winston-Smith took her place in the coupé beside her granddaughter, and until the carriage was turned and had started towards Fifth Avenue.

Then he crossed the broad space nearly to the

edge of the park and jumped on the first car that
came rushing around the curve. The platform
was crowded, but he took no heed of the men
who were pressed against him.

His thoughts were elsewhere and his heart was
full of hope : it was attuned to the gladness of
the spring-time. He did not see the young men
and maidens who flocked thickly up Broadway ;
he saw Winifred only ; he saw her face, her eyes,
her smile of welcome. He was to see her again,
at once almost, and he could tell her then how he
loved her, and he could ask her if she would not
try to love him. What if the only chance he
should have was in the street itself ? Only the
proposal itself was of importance, the place mattered nothing. Perhaps the unconventionality of
the proceeding even added zest to it. There was
unconventionality in the frankness with which
she had made the appointment. It was this
frankness partly which made his heart leap with
hope, and partly it was the welcome he thought
he had read in her eyes when their glances met
first.

The car sped on its way, stopping at almost
every corner to take on and to let off men and
women, who brushed against Harry Grant and
whom he did not see, so absorbed was he in
going over every word of his brief dialogue with
the girl he loved. On the sidewalks were thick
throngs of brightly dressed women looking into
the windows of the shops, where were displayed

brilliant parasols and trim yachting costumes
and summer stuffs in lightsome colors.

As the car crossed Fifth Avenue he saw the
carriage of Mrs. Winston-Smith only a block
away.   He recognized the coachman upright
on the box, and then all at once he wondered
what the coachman must have thought of his
talk through the open window, and of his abrupt
appearance.   He smiled — indeed he laughed
gently—for what did he care what the coachman
might think, or anybody else ?   It was what she
thought which was of importance, and nothing
else mattered at all.   And again he was seized
with impatience to see her once and to tell her
that he loved her, and to get her answer.   The
car was going swiftly, but it seemed to him to
crawl.   The coachman on the avenue was driv-
ing briskly, but Harry Grant was ready to re-
buke the man for his sluggishness.

At last the car passed the door of the florist's
Winifred had described.   Its window was filled
with azaleas massed with an artistic instinct almost Japanese.   Harry Grant rode to the corner
above and walked back very slowly, loitering
before a shop window, but wholly unconscious
of the spring neck-wear therein displayed.   Two
minutes later he saw Mrs. Winston-Smith's
carriage coming down Twenty-ninth Street.   It
turned into Broadway and stopped before the florist's wide window.   Mrs. Winston-Smith got out
and ordered the coachman to wait at the corner.

She had disappeared inside the florist's before
the coupé drew up in the side street.

As the coachman reined in his horses Harry
Grant stepped up to the open window.

"Winifred—" he began.

"Oh!" she cried, "you are here already?"
and again the blush crossed her face.

"Winifred," he repeated, leaning his head inside the carriage, "I may have only a minute to
say what I have to say, and I know this isn't the
right place to say it, either, but I have no choice,
for I may not have another chance. I have
waited so long that I simply must speak now."

He paused for a moment. She said nothing,
but she rubbed the back of her glove as though
to wear away a speck of dirt.

"Winnie," he went on, "what I want to say
is simple enough. I love you. Surely you must
know that?"

"Yes," she answered, raising her eyes to his,
"I know that."

"Then it's easier for me to go on. You know
me: you know all about me; you know all my
faults, or most of them anyway; you know I
love you. Do you think you could ever love me
a little in return? I will try so hard to deserve
it. I've been working ever since I was seventeen to make money enough to be able to ask
you to marry me. I've got a good position now,
one that I'm not ashamed to ask you to share.
Will you? Will you marry me, Winnie?"

Before she could make any answer, Harry Grant heard the voice of Mrs. Winston-Smith behind him saying to the coachman, "Home!"

He stepped back and found himself face to face with her.

"It's Mr. Grant, isn't it?" she said, with a haughty inclination of her head. "It's very good of you to amuse Winifred while I was in the shop. I'd ask you to come and have a cup of tea with us, but we are off to Tuxedo. And we sail on Tuesday; perhaps Winifred told you."

She stood there, expecting him to open the carriage door for her. It was the least he could do, and he did it. But he could find no words to respond to her conventional conversation. He looked at Winifred, and he saw that the color was deepening on her cheeks, and that her eyes were very bright.

"Grandma," she said, when at last Mrs. Winston-Smith was seated beside her—"Grandma," she repeated, loud enough for the young man to hear as he stood by the open window, "Harry has asked me to marry him—and you came out just before I had time to tell him that I would!"

(1895)

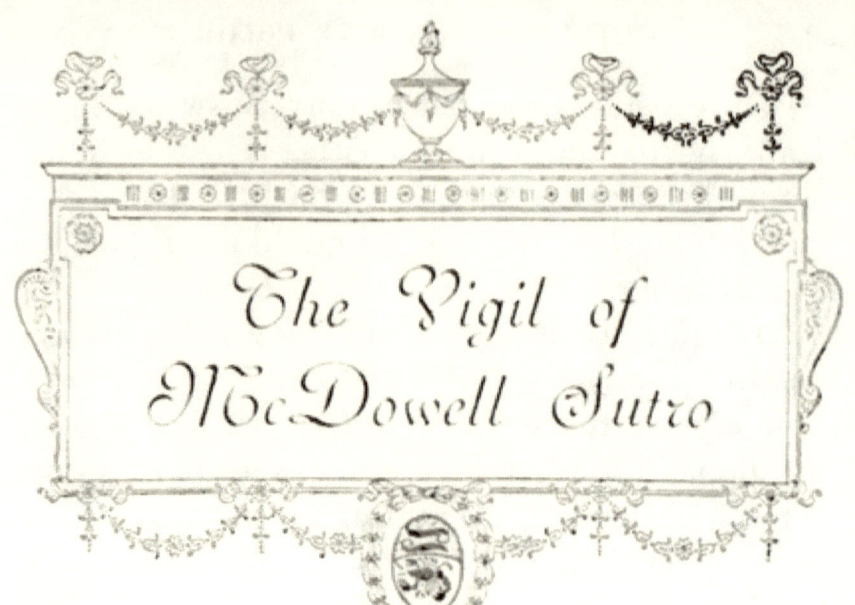

The Vigil of McDowell Sutro

OR the third time that afternoon the young man stood before the window of the post-office to ask the same question and to receive the same answer:

"Has any letter come for McDowell Sutro?"

"No."

This time he persisted, for he could not take no for an answer at that late hour of the day.

"Are you sure?" he asked, urgently.

"Certain sure," was the answer that came through the window.

"Will there be another mail from California to-night?" he inquired, clutching a last hope.

"Not to-night," responded the clerk.

The young man stood there for a second, staring unconsciously into the window, and not seeing anybody or anything. Then he turned slowly to go.

The clerk knew that look on the face of men who asked for letters, and he had a movement of kindness.

"Say, young feller!" he called, brusquely.

McDowell Sutro faced about instantly, with a swift flash of hope.

"If you're expecting money in that letter,

maybe it's registered," suggested the clerk.
"Ask over there in the corner."

"Thank you," the young man answered, grate-
fully; and he walked to the window in the corner with expectation again lighting his face.

But there was no registered letter for McDowell Sutro, and there could none arrive before
the next morning. And as the handsome young
Californian left the post-office he knew that he
had hardly a right even to hope that the letter
he was asking for should ever arrive.

He stepped out on Fifth Avenue; and though
a warm June wind blew balmily up from Washington Square, his heart was chill within him.
He shivered as he wondered what he was to do
now. He knew no one in New York, and he
had not a cent in his pocket.

In his youth he had expected to inherit a fortune, and so he learned no trade and studied no
profession. He had taught himself how to be
idle elegantly; he had never planned how to earn
his own living. Perhaps this was the reason why
he had failed to find any work to do during the
two gliding weeks since he had suddenly been
brought face to face with his final ten-dollar bill.

He had no more resources than he had friends.
His trunk, with the little clothing he owned, was
still at the boarding-house he had left ten days before; it was held by the landlady till he paid her
what he owed. His modest jewelry had been
pawned, bit by bit.

It was now about seven in the evening, and he had had no food since the coffee and cakes taken perhaps twelve hours earlier, and bought with the last dime left him after he had paid for his night's lodging. Having walked all day, he was weary and hungry, and he had no idea how he could get a roof over his head once again or fill his stomach once more. He had heard of men and women starving to death in the streets of New York, and he found himself inquiring if that were to be his fate.

Not guiding his steps consciously, he went up Fifth Avenue to the corner of Fourteenth Street, and then turned towards Broadway. The long June day was drawing to an end. Behind his back the red sun was settling down slowly. The street was crowded with cars and with carts; and people hurried along, eager to be with their families, and giving no attention to the homeless young man they brushed against.

When he came to Broadway it seemed to him as though the rush and the tumult redoubled, and as though the men and the women who passed him were being tossed to and fro by invisible breakers. The roar of the city rose all about him; it smote on his tired ears like the deafening crash of the surf after a northeaster. He likened himself to a spent swimmer about to have the life beaten out of him by the pounding of the waves, and certain sooner or later to be cast up on the beach, a stripped and bruised corpse.

So vividly did he picture this that involuntarily he straightened himself and drew a long breath. He was a good-looking young fellow, with a graceful brown mustache curling over his weak mouth. As he stood there, erect as though ready to fight for his life, more than one woman passing briskly along the street let his figure fill her eye with pleasure.

The cable-cars whisked around the curves before him, and beyond them he beheld the green fairness of Union Square. The freshness of its foliage as he saw it through the darksome twilight attracted him. He crossed cautiously, keeping a sharp lookout for the cars, and smiling as he noted how careful he was of his life, now he did not know how he was to sustain it.

As he stood at last in the verdant oasis in the centre of the square, suddenly the electric light whitewashed the pavement, and his unexpected shadow lay black and sprawling under his feet. He looked up, startled, and he saw the infinite arch of the sky curving over him—clear, cloudless, and illimitable. The faint sickle of the new moon hung low on the horizon. A towering building thrust its thin height into the air, and the yellow lights in its upper windows seemed like square panels inlaid in the deep blue of the sky. The beauty of the moment lifted him out of his present misery, and he was glad to be alive. The plash of the fountain fell on his ears and charmed them. The broad leaves of the aquatic plants swayed languidly as a gentle breeze blew across the surface of the water.

With a sigh of relief. McDowell Sutro dropped upon one of the park benches. Until he sat down he did not know how tired he was. His feet ached, and his stomach cried for food. And yet he was stout of heart. "If I've got to spend a night *à la belle étoile*," he said to himself, "I could have no better luck. There are beautiful stars a-plenty this evening. It's like that night in Venice when Tom Pixley and I took the two Morton girls out in our gondolas, and their aunt couldn't find us. I remember we had had a good dinner at Florian's, with an immense dish of *risotto milanese*—so big we had to leave some. I wish I had the chance again. I could finish it now if it was twice as much."

Over on Fourth Avenue, behind the equestrian statue of George Washington, there was a Hungarian restaurant, and from his bench at the edge of the grass McDowell Sutro could see the table right in the window at which an old man and a young woman were having dinner. He could follow every movement of their hands; he could count every mouthful they ate. At last he could bear it no longer, and he changed his seat to a bench nearer Broadway. Here he found himself facing another eating-room, in the broad windows of which many kinds of food were alluringly displayed. Men came out and lingered in the door-way long enough to light a cigarette.

7

When McDowell Sutro noted this, the craving for tobacco seized him. A smoke would not stay his stomach, but it would be a solace none the less. He rose to his feet and felt in all his pockets, in the vain hope that his fingers might touch some overlooked fragment of a cigar. There was something at the bottom of one of the pockets of his coat, but it mocked him by revealing itself as a match. He sank down on the bench and turned his eyes away from the restaurant, for he could not bear to gaze on the cakes and pies piled up behind the plate-glass, or to observe the smoke curling up from the lips of men who had eaten and drunk abundantly.

There was a bar-room under the hotel on the corner of Broadway, and every now and then two or three men pushed inside the swinging doors, to reappear five or ten minutes later. Farther down Broadway stood a theatre, and there was now a throng about its broad door-way. Another theatre faced the square, gay with prismatic signs and besprinkled with electric lights. McDowell Sutro watched men and women step up to the box-office of this place of amusement and buy their tickets and disappear within. He wondered why these men and women should have money to spare on a show, when he had not enough to pay for a meal and a night's lodging.

Perhaps it was the fatigue of his useless day, and perhaps it was the hypnotic influence of the revolving lights before the variety theatre, which caused the lonely young man to fall asleep. How long he slept he did not know, nor what waked him at last. But he had a doubtful memory of a human touch upon his body, and three of his pockets were turned inside out. When he discovered this, he laughed outright. The attempt to rob him then struck him as the funniest thing that had ever happened.

He must have slept for two or three hours at least, for the appearance of the square had changed. It was no longer evening: it was now night. While he looked about him he saw the doors of the theatre in Broadway pushed open, and the audience began to pour forth. A few moments later little knots of the play-goers passed him, still laughing with remembrance of the farce they had been witnessing. In another quarter of an hour the people began to come out of the other theatre, the variety show on the square, and the lights that flared above the doorway went out, all at once.

It was nearly midnight when two men sat down on the bench of which McDowell Sutro had been the sole occupant hitherto. They were tall and thin, both of them: they were clean-shaven; their clothes were shabby; and yet they carried themselves with an indescribable air, as though they were accustomed to brave the gaze of the world.

"No," said the elder of the two, continuing

their conversation, "she's no good. She has a figure like a flat-iron and a voice like a fog-horn, hasn't she? Well, there's no draft in that, is there? She's a Jonah, that's what she is, and she'd hoo-doo any show. Why, the last time I was on the road she tried to queer my act. I called her down right there and then, and when the star backed her up, I was going to give my two weeks' notice; and I'd have done it, too, but I was playing cases then, and I didn't want to come back here walking on my uppers. But if I had quit, they'd have closed in a month, I tell you! They didn't know who was drawing the money to their old show; but I did! You ought to have been in the one-night towns on the oil circuit and heard me do Shamus O'Brien. That used to fetch 'em every night— I tell you it did! And it used to make her tired!"

"Did you ever see me play Laertes?" asked the younger. "I did it first in 'Frisco in '72, when Larry Barrett came out there. Well, while I was on the stage with him, Hamlet didn't get a hand. I've got a notice here now that said I was the Greatest Living Laertes."

"I played Iago once with Larry Barrett," said the first speaker, "and I gave them such a realistic impersonation they used to hiss me off the stage almost."

"Have a cigarette?" asked the other, holding out a package.

"Don't care if I do," was the answer. "I've got a match."

"That's lucky, for I haven't," said the owner of the cigarettes.

"Well, I haven't, after all," the elder actor had to confess, after a vain search in his pockets.

"Let me provide the match," broke in McDowell Sutro. "I've only one, but it's at your service."

"Thank you," was the response. "Can I not offer you a cigarette?"

"I don't care if I do," the young man answered, involuntarily repeating the phrase he had just heard, as he thrust out his hand eagerly.

The first whiff of the smoke was like meat and drink to him; and in the sensuous enjoyment of the luxury he almost neglected to respond to the remark addressed to him. But in a minute he found himself chatting with the two actors pleasantly. Although they had been to California more than once, they knew none of his friends; but it cheered merely to hear again the names of familiar landmarks. There was more than a suggestion of haughtiness in the way they both condescended to him; but he did not resent this, even if he remarked it. Human companionship was sweet to him; and to drop into a chat with casual strangers on a bench in Union Square at midnight, even this diminished the desolation of his loneliness.

The talk lasted perhaps a quarter of an hour,

and then the two other men rose to go.   Mc-
Dowell Sutro stood up also, as though he were
at home and they were his guests.

"Come over and have a drink," said the elder
of the two.

And again the young man answered, "I don't
care if I do."

He would rather have had food than drink,
but he could not tell two strangers that he was
hungry.

As they passed before the statue of Lafay-
ette and crossed the car tracks, he wondered
whether the saloon where they were going to
was one of those which set out a free lunch.

When they entered the bar-room his eyes swept
it wolfishly, and then fixed themselves at the
end of the counter, where there were broad
dishes with cheese and crackers and sandwiches.
He could hardly control himself ; he wanted to
rush there and snatch the food and devour it.
But shame kept him standing near the door with
the two actors, though his gaze was fastened on
the dishes only a few feet from him.

The barkeeper set the bottle before them, and
they poured out the liquor.   Then they looked
at each other and said, "How !"

The elder actor half finished his drink at a
single gulp.   As he set down his glass he caught
McDowell Sutro staring at the free lunch.

"That's not a bad idea," he said, moving along
the bar — "not half bad.   I'll take a sandwich

myself. I feel a bit hollow to-night. I got three
encores after I gave them the 'Pride of Battery
B,' and I need something to build me up. Have
a sandwich?"

"I don't care if I do," responded the hungry
man, as his fingers closed on the bread. Yet when
he took the first mouthful it almost choked him.

Five minutes later he had said good-night to
his two chance acquaintances and he was again
back in the square. The scant food he had been
able to take lay hard in his stomach, and the
liquor he had drunk, little as that was also, was
yet enough to make his head whirl. He did not
walk unsteadily, although he was conscious that
it took an effort for him to carry himself without swerving.

The bench on which he had been sitting was
now occupied by four very young men in evening dress, who were gravely smoking pipes, as
though they were trying to acquire a taste for
this novel pastime. So he went to the centre
of the square, where he stood for a while looking
at the aquatic plants and listening to the spurtle
of the fountain.

All the seats around the fountain were occupied by men and women, most of whom seemed to
have settled themselves for the night, as though
they were used to sleeping there. McDowell
Sutro found himself speculating whether he, too,
would soon be accustomed to spending his nights
in the open air, without a roof over him.

One solid German had fallen into a slumber
so heavy that his snore became a loud snort.
Then a gray-coated policeman waked the sleeper
by smiting the soles of his feet with the club.

"This park ain't no bedroom." said the policeman. "and I ain't goin' to have you fellows
goin' to sleep here either! See?"

After walking three or four times around on
the outer circle of the little park, the young man
found a vacant seat on a bench near the corner
of Broadway and Seventeenth Street. The brilliantly lighted cable-cars still glided swiftly up
and down Broadway with their insistent gongs,
but they were now fewer and fewer; and the
cross-town horse-cars passed only two or three
an hour. The long day of the city was nearly
over at last, and for the two or three hours before dawn there would be peace and a cessation
of the struggle.

As he sat back on the bench, sick with weariness, the occupant of the seat next to him aroused
herself. She was an elderly woman, with grizzled
hair.

"I beg your pardon—if I waked you up?"
said the young man.

"You did wake me up." she answered, "but
I forgive you. It's only cat-naps I get anyway
nowadays. I haven't stretched my legs out between the sheets and had my fill of sleep for a
month of Sundays. And I'm a glutton for sleeping if I've the chance. But I'm getting used to

sitting up late," and she laughed without bitterness. "What time is it now?" she asked.

McDowell Sutro involuntarily lifted his hand to the pocket of his waistcoat, and then he dropped it quickly. Blushing, he answered, "I don't know—I—"

"Time's up, isn't it?" she returned, with a laugh of understanding. "I haven't got my watch with me either; I left it in my other clothes at my uncle's. But Mr. Tiffany is a kind-hearted man, and he keeps a clock all lighted up for us to see. Your eyes are younger than mine—what time is it now?"

McDowell Sutro looked intently for half a minute before he could make out the hour. At last he answered, "It's almost half-past one, I think."

"Then I've a couple of hours for another nap before the sparrows wake us all up," she returned. "Is it the first night you have come to this hotel of ours?"

"Yes," he replied.

"I thought so," she continued, "by your feeling for your watch. You'll get out of the way of doing that soon."

His face blanched with fear that she might be predicting the truth. Would the time ever come when he should be used to sleeping in the open air?

The old woman turned a little, so that she could look at him.

"It's a handsome young fellow you are," she went on; "there's more than one house in town where they'd take you in on your looks — and tuck you up in bed, too, and keep you warm."

"Perhaps I'm better off here." he remarked, feeling that he was expected to say something.

"This isn't a bad hotel of ours, this isn't." she returned; "it's well ventilated, for one thing. Of course you can go to the station-house if you want. I don't. I've tried it, and I'd sooner sleep in the snow than in the station-house, with the creatures you meet there. This hotel of ours here keeps open all night; and it's on the European plan, I'm thinking—leastwise you can have anything you can pay for. When the owl-wagon is here, you can get a late supper—if you have the price of it. I haven't."

"Neither have I," he answered.

"Then there's two of us ready for an invite to breakfast." she responded, cheerily. "If any one asks us, it's no previous engagement will make us decline, I'm thinking."

He made no answer, for his heart sank as he looked into the future.

"Are you hungry now?" she asked.

"Yes," he answered, simply.

"So am I," she replied, "and I can't get used to it. Hunger is like pain, isn't it? It don't let go of you: it don't get tired and let up on you. It's a stayer, that's what it is, and it keeps right on attending strictly to business. Sometimes, when I'm very hungry, I feel like committing suicide, don't you?"

"No," he responded—"at least, not yet: I haven't had enough of life to be tired of it so soon."

"Neither have I," was her answer. "Sometimes I'm ready to quit, but somehow I don't do it. But it would be so easy: you throw yourself in front of one of those cable-cars coming down Broadway now—and you'll get rapid transit to kingdom come. But they don't sell excursion tickets. Besides, being crunched by a cable-car is a dreadful mussy way of dying, don't you think? And to-day's Friday, too—and I don't believe I'd ever have any luck in the next world if I was to commit suicide on a Friday."

"This isn't Friday any longer," he suggested; "it's Saturday morning."

"So it is now," she rejoined; "then we'd better be getting our beauty-sleep as soon as we can, for the flower-market here will wake us up soon enough, seeing it's Saturday. And so, good-night to you!"

"Good-night!" he responded.

"And may you dream you've found a million dollars in gold, and then wake up and find it true!" she continued.

"Thank you," he replied, wondering what manner of woman his neighbor might be.

She said nothing more, but settled herself

again and closed her eyes. She was dressed in
rusty black, and she had a thin black shawl over
her head. She had been a very handsome woman—so she impressed the young man by her side
—and he was wholly at a loss to guess how she
came to be here, in the street, at night, without
money and alone. She seemed out of place there;
for her manner, though independent, was not
defiant. There was no rasping harshness in her
tones; indeed, her talk was dashed with jovial-
ity. Her speech even puzzled him, although he
thought that showed her to be Irish.

Turning these things over in his mind, he fell
asleep. He dreamed the same dream again and
again—a dream of a barbaric banquet, where
huge outlandish dishes were placed on the table
before him. The savor of them was strange to
his nostrils, but it brought the water to his
mouth. Then, when he made as though to help
himself and stay his appetite, the whole feast
slid away beyond his reach, and finally faded
into nothing. The dream differed in detail
every time he dreamed it; and the last time the
only dish on the board before him was a gigantic
pasty, which he succeeded in cutting open, only
to behold four-and-twenty blackbirds fly forth.
The birds circled about his head, and then returned to the empty shell of the pasty, and
perched there, and sang derisively.

So loudly did they sing that McDowell Sutro
awoke, and he heard in the trees above him and

THE VIGIL OF McDOWELL SUTRO   109

behind him the chirping and twittering of count-
less sparrows.

He recalled what the old woman had said—
that the birds would wake them up. Probably
they had aroused her first, for the place on the
bench next to him was empty.

He rose to his feet and looked about him. It
was almost daybreak, and already there were
rosy streaks in the eastern sky. A squirrel was
running up and down a large tree in the middle
of the grass-plot behind the bench on which he
had been sleeping. In the open space at the
northern end of the square there were a dozen
or more gardeners' wagons, thick with growing
flowers in pots, and men were arranging these
plants in rows upon the pavement. Another
heavy wagon, loaded with roses only, rolled across
the car track and disturbed a flock of pigeons
that swirled aloft for a moment and then settled
down again. A moist breeze blew up from the
bay, and brought a warning of rain to come later
in the day.

The sleepers on the other benches here and
there throughout the square were waking, one
by one. McDowell Sutro saw one of them go to
the drinking-fountain and wash his hands and
face. He followed this example as best he could.
When he had made an end of this his eye fell
on Tiffany's clock, which told the hour of half-
past four. A few minutes later the first rays of
the sun began to gild the cornices of the tall

buildings which towered above the Lincoln statue.

Within the next hour and a half the cable-cars began to pass down-town more frequently, and the cross-town cars from the ferries also came closer together. The gardeners' wagons and the plants taken from them filled the broad space at the upper end of the square. Milk-carts rattled across the car tracks that bounded the square on all four sides. The signs of the coming day multiplied, and McDowell Sutro noted them all, one after another, with unfailing interest, despite the gnawing pain in his stomach. It was the first time he had ever seen the awakening of a great city.

He walked away from Union Square as far as Fifth Avenue and Twenty-third Street, and again as far as Third Avenue and Fourteenth Street; but he found himself always returning to the flower-market. At last a hope sprang up within him. Among the purchasers were ladies not strong enough to carry home the heavy pots, and perhaps he might pick up a job. This was not the way he wanted to earn his daily bread, but never before had he felt the want of the daily bread so keenly.

When he came back to the line of gardeners' wagons he found other men out of work also hanging about in the hope of making an honest penny; and more than once he saw one or another of these others sent away, burdened with tall plants.

At last he took his courage in his hand, and went up to a little old lady whom he had seen going from row to row. She had bright eyes and a gentle manner and a kindly smile. He asked her, if she bought anything, to let him carry it home for her. She looked at the handsome young fellow, and her glance was as shrewd as it seemed to him sympathetic.

"Yes," she answered, "I think I can trust you."

A minute or two later she bargained with a Scotch gardener for two azaleas in full bloom. Then she turned to McDowell Sutro:

"Will you take those to the Post-Graduate Hospital, corner of Second Avenue and Twentieth Street, for half a dollar?"

"Yes," he answered, eagerly.

"Very well," she responded. "They are for the Babies' Wards. Say that they are from Miss Van Dyne. The Babies' Wards, you understand? And here is your money. I've got to trust you; but you have an honest face, and I don't believe that you would rob sick children of the sight and smell of the flowers they love."

"No," said McDowell Sutro. "I wouldn't." He picked up the heavy pots, and held one in the hollow of each arm. "The Babies' Wards of the Post - Graduate Hospital, from Miss Van Dyne? Is that it?"

"That's it," she answered, with her illuminating smile.

He walked off with the plants. Having the
money in his pocket to break his fast, it seemed
as though he could not get to the hospital swiftly
enough. But when he had handed in the flowers,
and was on his way back again to the square, he
remembered suddenly the woman who had sat
by him on the bench, and who had been hungry
also. He had fifty cents in his pocket now, and
in the window of an eating-house on Fourth
Avenue he saw the sign, "Regular Breakfast, 25
cts." He had money enough to buy two regular
breakfasts, one for himself and one for her.

He made the circle of the little park three
times, besides traversing it in every direction,
and then he had to confess that she was beyond
his reach.

So he went to the restaurant alone, and had a
regular breakfast all to himself.

When he came forth he felt refreshed, and the
people who were now hurrying along the streets
struck him as happier than those he had seen in
the gray dawn. The long sunbeams were lighting the side streets. The workmen with their
dinner-pails were giving place to the shop-girls
with their luncheons tied up in paper.

The roar of the great city arose once more as
the mighty tide of humanity again swept through
its thoroughfares.

He went back to the gardeners' wagons, believ-
ing that he might earn another half-dollar. But
when he saw other men waiting there hungrily,

"THE PEOPLE STRUCK HIM AS HAPPIER"

he turned away, thinking it only fair to give them a chance too.

He found a seat in the sun. and looked on while the flower-market was stripped by later purchasers. He wondered where the plants were all going, and then he remembered that the same flowers serve for the funeral and for the wedding. For the first time it struck him as strange that the plant which dresses a dinner-table to-day may gladden a sick-room to-morrow, and be bedded on a grave the day after.

At last he thought the hour had come when the post-office would be open again, and he set off for Fifth Avenue and Thirteenth Street.

When he reached the station he checked his walk. He did not dare go in, although the doors were open, and he could see other men and women asking questions at the little square windows. What if his questions should meet with the same answer as yesterday? What if he should have to spend another night in Union Square?

He nerved himself at last and entered. As he approached the window the clerk looked at him with a glance of recognition.

"McDowell Sutro, isn't it? Yes—there *is* a letter for you. Overweight, too—there's four cents extra postage to pay."

The young man's hand trembled as he put down the quarter left after paying for his regular breakfast. He seized the envelope swiftly, and almost forgot to pick up his change, till the clerk reminded him of it.

He tore the letter open. It was from Tom Pixley; it contained a post-office order for fifty dollars; and it began:

"My Dear Mac,—Go and see Sam Sargent, 78 Broadway, and he will get you a place on the surveyor's staff for the new line of the Barataria Central. I'm writing to him by this mail, and—"

But for a minute McDowell Sutro could read no further. His eyes had filled with tears.

(1895)

An Irrepressible Conflict

THE summer sun had blazed down all day on the low wooden roof of the old shed lately used as an ice-cream saloon, and now hastily altered to accommodate a post of the Salvation Army. Placards at the wide doorway proclaimed that All were Welcome, and besought the stranger to Come in and be Saved. The tall tenements that lined the side-streets east and west had emptied their hundreds of inhabitants out into the avenue that evening, and the sidewalks were thronged with men and women languid from the heat of the day, and longing for the lazy breeze that sometimes creeps into the city with nightfall; but few of them cared to enter the stifling hall where the song-service was about to begin, and that night especially there were many counter-attractions out-doors. Already were the rockets beginning to burst far above the square where the fireworks were to be displayed; and now and again a boy (who had more than boyish self-control) produced a reserve pack of fire-crackers, and dropped them into a barrel, and capered away with delight as the owner of the barrel was called to his door by the rattle of their explosion.

A pale and thin young woman, in the uniform

of the Salvation Army, stood wearily in the entrance, proffering the *War Cry* to all those who came near. She looked as though she had been pretty when she was a girl. Now she was obviously worn and weak, like one recovering from a long illness. High up over her head appeared a shower of colored stars shot forth from a bomb; and then she remembered how she had seen the fireworks on the last Fourth of July, only a year before, lying on her bed which Jim had pulled to the window before he went down to conduct the meeting. She had lain there peacefully with her two-weeks-old baby in her arms, and it had seemed to her as though the glowing wheels that revolved in the air, and the curving lines of fire that rose and fell again, were but a prefiguration of a golden future where all would be splendor and glory. How that vision had faded into blackness in the months that followed!—when the baby sickened because they had not proper food for him, and when Jim broke down also; and she had had to get up, feeble as she was, and nurse them both until they died, one after another. When she let herself think of those days of despair, she had always to make a resolute effort if she did not wish to give way and go into a fit of sobbing that left her exhausted for the next twenty-four hours.

She mastered her rising emotion and turned for relief to the duty of the moment. For five minutes no one had bought a paper from her, and the time had come to go into the hall to take part in the service of song.

She pushed inside the swinging-door and found that perhaps a score of visitors had gathered, and that already half a dozen members of the Salvation Army had taken their seats at the edge of the low platform at the end of the shallow hall. Captain Quigley was standing there, with his shiny black hair carefully curled and his pointed beard carefully combed. He was waiting, ready to begin, with his accordion in his hands.

She wondered why it was that she was always sorry to have Captain Quigley lead the service. She would not deny that he led well, giving a swing to the tunes he played that carried all the people off their feet: he sang sweetly and he spoke feelingly. But she did not altogether like his manner, which was almost patronizing; and then he had a way of bringing her suddenly into his remarks and of calling her forward needlessly. Even after her two years' service she shrank from personalities and from self-exhibition. Yet there was no doubt that he meant to be kind to her, and she knew that he had allowed her special privileges more than once. With motherly kindness Adjutant Willetts had asked her only a week before if she really liked Captain Quigley, telling her that if she did not like him, she ought to be careful not to encourage him, and since that talk with the adjutant her distaste for the captain had been intensified.

It was as though Captain Quigley had been
waiting for her to appear, for he began to speak
as soon as he saw her.   In a high nasal voice and
with an occasional elided aspirate, he welcomed
those present and told them he was glad that
they had come.   He asked them all to take part
in singing the grand old hymn, "There Is a
Fountain Filled with Blood."   He set the tune
with his accordion, and lined out the first stanza
and led in the singing.   Only three or four of the
chance visitors joined in the song, the burden
of which was borne by the members of the Salvation Army.

Then the captain told his hearers that there
was a new *War Cry* published that very morning full of interesting things, and containing the
words of the songs they would all sing later, so
he wanted everybody in the hall to buy one, that
they could all follow the music.

The thin young woman with the saddened
face began to move down the aisles offering her
papers right and left.

"That's the way, Sister Miller," called out the
captain, as though to encourage her ; but she
winced as she heard her name thus thrown to
the public.   " I want you all to buy Sister Miller's
papers, so that she can come up here and join us
in the singing.   You don't know what a sweet
voice Sister Miller has—but we know."

He continued to talk thus familiarly as she
made the circuit of the seats.   When she had

taken her place on the platform by the side of Adjutant Willetts, who smiled at her with maternal affection in her eye. then suddenly the captain changed his tone. " Now we will ask the Lord to bless us—to bless us all, to bless this meeting. I don't know why any of you have come here to-night, but I do know this : if you have come here for God's blessing, you will get it. If you have come here for something else, I don't know whether you will get it : but if you have come here for that you will surely get it. God always gives His blessing to all who ask for it. Brother Higginson, will you lead us in prayer ?"

The men and women on the platform fell on their knees, and the most of those scattered about the hall bowed their heads reverently, while Brother Higginson prayed that the blessing of God might descend upon them that night. Sister Miller had heard Brother Higginson lead in prayer many times and she knew almost to a word what he was likely to say, for the range of his appeal was limited : but she always thrilled a little at the simple fervor of the man. It annoyed her, as usual, to have the captain punctuate the appeal of Brother Higginson with an occasional " Amen ! Amen !" or " Hallelujah !"

After the prayer there was another gospel song, and then the captain laid aside his accordion and took up a Bible. He read a passage from the Old Testament describing the advance

of the Children of Israel into the desert, guided
by a pillar of cloud by day and a pillar of fire
by night.   He held the book in his hand while
he expounded his text.   The Children of Israel
had their loins girded to fight the good fight, he
said.   That is what every people has to do ; the
Israelites had to do it, the English had to do
it, the Americans had to do it.   They all knew
what the Fourth of July stood for and how well
Americans fought then, more than a hundred
years ago; and so saying he seized the flag which
had been leaning against the wall behind him,
by the side of the blood-red banner of the Salvation Army.

As he was waving the Stars and Stripes Sister
Miller felt her dislike accentuated, for she knew
that the captain was an Englishman who had
been here but a few years, and it seemed to her
mean of him to be taking sides against his native
land.   She wondered if he was really ignorant
enough to think that one of the great battles of
the Revolution had been fought on the Fourth of
July.

Then her mind went back to her girlhood, and
she recalled the last celebration of the Fourth
that had taken place in the old school-house at
home the summer before she graduated.   She
remembered how old Judge Standish read the
Declaration of Independence with a magnificent
air of proprietorship, as though he had just
dashed it off.   Other incidents of that day came

floating back to her memory as she sat there in
the thick air of the little hall, and she ceased to
hear Captain Quigley calling urgently on all those
present to be Soldiers of God. In her ears there
echoed, instead, the pleading words of young
Dexter Standish, telling her that he was going to
the Naval Academy and that he wanted her to
wait for him till he should come back. She had
given her promise, and why had she not kept her
word? Why had she been foolishly jealous when
she heard that he was the best dancer in his class
at Annapolis, and that all the Baltimore girls
were wild to dance with him. She had long ago
discovered that her reason for breaking off the
engagement was wholly inadequate; and, in her
folly, she had not foreseen that Dexter could not
leave the Academy and come to her and explain.
If only he had presented himself and told her he
loved her she would have forgiven him, even if
he had really deserved punishment. But he was
a cadet, and he would not have a leave of absence
for another year. Before that year was out, she
had married James Miller, a theological student,
who soon threw up all his studies in his religious
zeal to join the Salvation Army, as though craving martyrdom. Jim had loved her, and he had
thought she loved him. It was with a swift pang
of reproach that she found herself asking whether it was not better for Jim that he had died
before he found out that his wife did not love
him as he loved her.

With the ingenuity that came of long experience, Captain Quigley had ended his address with
a quotation from "Onward, Christian Soldiers,"
and Sister Miller was roused from her reverie to
take part in the chorus. When they had sung
three stanzas the captain stopped abruptly and
turned to the gray-haired woman who sat beside
Sister Miller, and called on Adjutant Willetts to
say a few words of loving greeting to the souls
waiting to be saved.

To Sister Miller it was a constant delight to be
with the adjutant, to be comforted by her motherly smile and to be sustained by her cheerful
faith. There was a Quaker simplicity about Sister Willetts, and a Quaker strength of character
that the wan and worn Sister Miller had found
she could always rely upon. And another characteristic of the elder woman's endeared her also
to the younger : her religious fervor was as fresh
as it was sincere, and she gave her testimony night
after night with the same force and the same
feeling that she had given it the first time. Too
many of the others had reduced what they had to
say to a mere formula, modified but little and
delivered at last in almost mechanical fashion.
But Sister Willetts stood forward on the platform
and bore witness to her possession of the peace of
God which passeth all understanding : and she did
this most modestly, with neither shyness nor tim-
idity, merely as though she were doing her duty
gladly in declaring what God had done for her.

When the adjutant had made an end of speaking and had taken her seat by the side of the pale young woman, who smiled back at her again. Captain Quigley grasped his accordion once more.

"Now you shall have a solo," he said. "Sister Miller will sing that splendid old hymn, 'Rock of Ages.' Come. Sister Miller."

Her voice had no great power, but it sufficed for that little hall. She did not like to stand forward conspicuously, but the singing itself she always enjoyed. Sometimes she was almost able to forget herself as she poured out her soul in song.

On that Fourth of July evening she had not more than begun when she became conscious that somebody was staring at her with an intensity quite different from the ordinary gaze of curiosity to which she was accustomed. She obeyed the impulse, and looked down into the eyes of Dexter Standish fixed upon her as though he had come to claim possession of her at once.

So unexpected was this vision. and so enfeebled was her self-control. that her voice faltered, and she almost broke off in the middle of a line. But she stiffened herself. and though she felt the blood dyeing her face. she sang on sturdily. Her first thought was to run away—to run away at once and hide herself, somewhere. anywhere, so that she were only out of his sight. He had not seen her for six years and more. and in those weary years she had lost her youth and her looks. She knew that she was no longer the pretty girl he had loved, and she shrank from his scrutiny of her faded features and of her shrunken figure.

She could not run away and she could not hide; she had to stand there and let him gaze at her and discover how old she looked and how worn. She met his eyes again—he never took them from her—and it seemed to her that they were full of pity. She resented this. What right had he to compassionate her? She drew her thin frame up and sang the louder in mere bravado. Yet she was glad when she came to the end, and was able to sink back into the seat by the side of Sister Willetts.

The captain spoke up at once, and said that the time had come to take up a collection. Let every man give a little, in proportion to his means, no more and no less. Would Sister Willetts and Sister Miller go about among the people to col-lect the offerings?

As she picked up her tambourine she turned impulsively to the elder woman.

"Let me go to those near the platform, please," she begged. "Won't you take the out-side rows?"

The adjutant looked down on her a little sur-prised, but agreed at once.

The younger woman went only a few steps down the aisles, keeping as far away from him as possible. Whenever she glanced towards him

she found his eyes fixed upon her, following her
everywhere ; and now it was not pity she thought
she saw in his look, but love—the same love she
had seen in those eyes the last time they two had
stood face to face.

When the tambourines had been extended towards everybody in the hall, the two women went
back to the platform and the adjutant counted
up the money—coppers and nickels, most of it,
and not two dollars in all.

The captain kept on steadfastly. He gave out
another hymn. When that had been sung. he
turned to a portly man who had come in late and
who was sitting on the platform behind Brother
Higginson.

"Brother Jackman." he asked, with unction,
"how is your soul to-night ? Can't you tell us
about it ?"

While the portly man. standing uneasily with
his hands on the chair before him, was briskly
setting forth the circumstances of his assured
salvation, Sister Miller was silent on the platform.

She could not help seeing Dexter Standish,
who was straight in front of her. She noted how
erect he was, and how resolutely his shoulders
were squared. She saw that he was older. too :
and she observed that his face had a masterful look, wanting there the last time she had
seen him.

He had always been a fine-looking fellow, and

the training at Annapolis had done him good. He
was no mere youth now, but a man, bronzed and
bearded, and bearing himself like one who knew
what he wanted and meant to get it. She real-
ized that the woman he chose to guard from the
world would be well shielded. A weary woman
might find rest under the shelter of his stalwart
protection. Involuntarily she contrasted the
man she had promised to marry with the man
she had married—the manly strength of the one
with the gentle weakness of the other. Then she
blushed again, for this seemed to her disloyalty to
the dead. Jim had been very good to her always ;
he was the father of her child ; he never did any
wrong. But the thought returned again—perhaps if he had had more force of character the
child need not have died as it did.

Brother Jackman was rattling along glibly, but
Sister Mille lid not heed him. She did not hear
him even. She did not hear anything distinctly
during the rest of the service. She rose to her
feet with the rest of them, and she sat down
again automatically, and she knelt like one in
a trance. When the meeting was over and the
people began to disperse she saw that he did not
move. He stood there silently, waiting for her
to come to him, ready to bear her away. Without a word Sister Miller knew what it was her
old lover wanted ; he wanted to pick up their
love-story where it had been broken off four years
before.

When the hall was nearly empty he started towards her.

She turned to the gray-haired woman by her side.

"Tell me what to do," she cried.   "He is coming to take me away with him."

Sister Willetts saw the young man advancing slowly, as those last to go made a path for him.

"Is he in love with you, too?" she asked.

"Yes," the younger woman answered.

"And do you love him?"

"Yes—at least. I think so.   Oh yes!"

"And is he a good man?" was the last question.

"Yes, indeed," came the prompt reply, "the best man I ever knew!"

The sturdy figure was drawing nearer and the elder woman rose.

"If you love him better than you love your work with us, go to him, in God's name," she said.   "We seek no unwilling workers here.   If you cannot give yourself to the service joyfully, putting all else behind you, go in peace—and may the blessing of God be with you!"

She bent forward and kissed the younger woman and left her, as Dexter Standish came and stood before her.

"Margaret," he said, firmly. "I have come for you."

Without a word she stepped down from the platform and went with him.

9

When they came to the door a hansom happened to pass and he called it.

" Where are you taking me ?" she asked, glad to be under the shelter of his devotion and ready to relinquish all right to decide upon her future for herself.

"To my mother," he answered, as he lifted her into the vehicle. "She's at a hotel here. She'll be glad to see you."

" Will she ?" the girl asked, doubtfully.

" Yes," was the authoritative answer, " she knows that I have always loved you."

(1897)

The Solo Orchestra

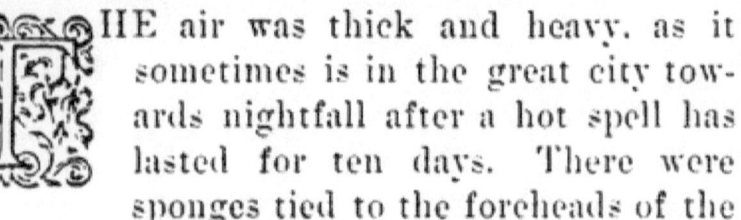THE air was thick and heavy, as it sometimes is in the great city towards nightfall after a hot spell has lasted for ten days. There were sponges tied to the foreheads of the horses that wearily tugged at the overladen crosstown cars. The shop-girls going home fanned themselves limply. The men released from work walked languidly, often with their coats over their arms. The setting sun burned fiery red as it sank behind the hills on the other side of the Hudson. But the night seemed likely to be as hot as the day had been, for the leaves on the trees were motionless now, as they had been all the afternoon.

We had been kept in town all through July by the slow convalescence of our invalid, and with even the coming of August we could not hope to get away for another ten days yet. The excessive heat had retarded the recovery of our patient by making it almost impossible for her to sleep. That evening, as it happened, she had dropped off into an uneasy slumber a little after six o'clock, and we had left her room gently in the doubtful hope that her rest might be prolonged for at least an hour.

I had slipped down-stairs and was standing
on the stoop, with the door open behind me,
when I heard the shrill notes of the Pan-pipes,
accompanied by the jingling of a set of bells
and the dull thumping of a drum. I understood
at once that some sort of wandering musician
was about to perform, and I knew that with the
first few bars the needful slumber of our invalid
would be interrupted violently.

I closed the door behind me softly and sprang
down the steps, and sped swiftly to the corner
around which the sounds seemed to proceed. If
the fellow is a foreigner, I thought, I must give
him a quarter and so bribe him to go away, and
then he will return every evening to be bought
off again, and I shall become a subscriber by
the week to the concerts I do not wish to hear.
But if the itinerant musician is an American,
of course I can appeal to him, as one gentleman
to another, and we shall not be troubled with him
again.

When I turned the corner I saw a strange
figure only a few yards distant—a strange figure most strangely accoutred—a tall, thin, loose-
jointed man, who had made himself appear taller
still by wearing a high-peaked hat, the pinna-
cle of which was surmounted by a wire frame-
work, in which half a dozen bells were suspended,
ringing with every motion of the head. He had
on a long linen duster, which flapped about his
gaunt shanks encased in tight, black trousers.

"THE AIR WAS THICK AND HEAVY"

Between his legs he had a pair of cymbals, fastened one to each knee. Upon his back was strapped a small bass-drum, on which there was painted the announcement that the performer was "Prof. Theophilus Briggs, the Solo Orchestra." A drumstick was attached to each side of the drum and connected with a cord that ran down his legs to his feet, so that by beating time with his toes he could make the drum take part in his concert. The Pan-pipes that I had heard were fastened to his breast just at the height of his chin, so that he could easily blow into them by the slightest inclination of his head. In his left hand he held a fiddle, and in his right hand he had a fiddle-bow. Just as I came in sight, he tapped the fiddle with the bow, as though to call the attention of the orchestra. Then he raised the fiddle; not to his chin, for the Pan-pipes made this impossible, but to the other position, not infrequent among street musicians, just below the shoulder. Evidently I had just arrived in time.

He was not a foreigner, obviously enough. It needed only one glance at the elongated visage, with its good-natured eyes and its gentle mouth, to show that here was a native American whose parents and grandparents also had been born on this side of the Atlantic.

"I beg your pardon for interrupting you before you begin," I said, hastily, "but I shall be very much obliged indeed if you would kindly

consent to give your performance a little farther
down this street—a little farther away from this
corner."

I saw at once that I had not chosen my words
adroitly, for the kindly smile faded from his lips,
and there was more than a hint of stiffness in
his manner as he responded, slowly :

"I don't know as I quite catch your meaning," he began.   "I ain't—"

"I'm sorry to have to ask you to go away," I
interrupted, wishing to explain; "I'd like to
hear your concert myself; but the fact is, there's
a member of my family slowly recovering from
a long sickness, and she's only just fallen asleep
now for the first time since midnight."

"Why didn't you say so at first ?" was Profess-
or Briggs's immediate response, and the genial
smile returned to his thin face.   "Of course, I
don't want to worry no one with my music. And
I'd just as lief as not go over the other side of
the city if it will be any more agreeable to a sick
person.   I know myself what it is to have sickness in the house ; there ain't no one knows what
that is better than I do—no one don't."

"It is very kind of you, I'm sure," I said, as
he walked back with me to the corner.

"Oh, that's all right," he returned.   "It don't
make any differ to me.   Now you just show me
which house it is, so I can keep away from it."

I pointed out the door to him.

"The third one from the corner, is it ?" he re-

peated. " Well, that's all right. And I am much
obliged to you for telling me about it. for I should
have hated to wake up a sick person : and these
pipes and this drum ain't exactly soothing to the
sick. are they ?"

Then the smile ripened to a laugh, and after I
had thanked him once more and shaken hands.
he turned back and walked away, accompanied
by the bevy of children who had encircled us ex-
pectantly ever since I had first spoken to him.

Before daybreak the next morning a storm
broke over the city. and the heavy rain kept up
all day. cooling the streets at last and washing
the atmosphere. With the passing of the hot
wave sleep became easier for us all. Men walked
to their offices in the morning with a brisker
step, and the shop - girls were no longer listless
as they went to their work. Our invalid im-
proved rapidly. and we could count the days
before we should be able to take her out of the
city.

The rain-storm had brought this relief on a
Thursday. and the skies did not clear till Friday
evening. The air kept its freshness over Saturday and Sunday.

On the latter day. towards nightfall. I had
taken my seat on the stoop. as is the custom of
New-Yorkers kept in town during the summer
months. I had brought out a cushion or two.
and I was smoking my second after-supper cigar.

I felt at peace with the world, and for the moment I had even dispensed with the necessity of thinking. It satisfied me to watch the rings of tobacco-smoke as they curled softly above my head.

Although I was thus detached from earth, I became at last vaguely conscious that a man had passed before the house for two or three times, and that as he passed he had stared at me as though he expected recognition. With his next return my attention was aroused. I saw that he was a tall, thin man, of perhaps fifty years of age, with a lean face clean-shaven, plainly dressed in black, and in what was obviously a Sunday suit, so revealing itself by its odd wrinkles and creases. As he came abreast of me, he slackened his gait and looked up. When he caught my eye he smiled. And then I recognized him at once. It was Professor Theophilus Briggs, the Solo Orchestra.

When he discovered that I knew him again he stood still. I rose to my feet and greeted him.

"I thought this was the house," he began, "but I wa'n't sure for certain. You see, my memory ain't any longer than a toad's tail. Still, I allowed I hadn't ought to disremember anything as big as a house—now had I?" and he laughed pleasantly. "And I thought that was you, too, setting up there on the porch," he went on, cheerfully. "And I'm glad it is, because I wanted to see you again to ask after the lady's health. Did she have her sleep out that evening? And how is she getting on now?"

I thanked him again for his considerate action the first time we had met, as well as for his kindly inquiries now, and I was glad to give him good news of our patient. Then I recognized the duties of hospitality, and I asked my visitor if he would not "take something."

"No, thank you," he returned—"that is, if there ain't no offence. Fact is, I've quit. I don't look on the wine when it is red now, for it biteth like an adder and it stingeth like a serpent, and I don't want any more snakes in mine. I've had enough of them, I have. Croton extra dry is good enough for me now, I guess; and I ain't no use now for a happy family of blue mice and green rats and yellow monkeys. I've had whole menageries of them, too, in my time— regular Greatest Show on Earth, you know, and me with a season ticket. But it's like all these continuous performances, you get tired of it pretty soon—leastways, I did, and so I quit, and I don't touch a drop now."

"Sworn off?" I suggested, as I made room for him on the cushion by my side.

"Oh no," he said, simply, as he sat down: "I hadn't no need to swear off. I just quit; that's all there was to it."

"Some men do not find it so very easy to give up drinking," I remarked.

"That's so, too," he answered, "and I didn't

either, for a fact. But I just had to do it, that's all. You see, I'd given drinking a fair show, and I'd found it didn't pay. Well, I don't like no trade where you're bound to lose in the long-run—seems a pretty poor way to do business, don't it? So I quit."

This seemed to call for a commonplace from me, and I was equal to the occasion. "It's easier to get into the way of taking a drop now and then than it is to get out of it."

"I got into it easy enough, I know that," he returned, smiling genially. "It was when I was in the army. After a man has been laying out in the swamp for a week or so, a little rum ain't such a bad thing to have in the house."

Then it was that for the first time I noticed the bronze button in his coat.

"So you were in the army?" I said, with the ever-rising envy felt by so many of my generation who lived through the long years of the Civil War mere boys, too young to take part in the struggle.

"I was a drummer-boy at Gettysburg," he answered; "and it warn't mighty easy for me, either."

"How so?" I asked.

"Well, it was this way," he explained. "Father, he was a Maine man, and he was a sea-captain. And when mother died, after a spell father he up and married again. Now that second wife of father's she didn't like me; and I didn't like

her either. not overmuch. I guess there warn't
no love lost between us. She liked to make a
voyage with father now and then, and so did
I. We was both with him on a voyage he
made about the time the war broke out. We
cleared for Cowes and a market, and along in
the summer of '62 we was in the Mediterranean.
It was towards the end of that summer we
come into Genoa, and there we got a chance at
the papers, all filled chock-full of battles. And
it didn't seem as though things was going any too
well over here, either, and so I felt I'd like to
come home and lend a hand in putting down the
rebellion. You see, I was past fourteen then,
and I was tall for my age—'most as tall as I am
now, I guess. I was doing a man's work on the
ship, and I didn't see why I couldn't do a man's
work in helping Uncle Sam, seeing he seemed to
be having a hard time of it. And I don't mind
telling you, too, that she had been making me
have considerable of a hard time of it, too ; and
there warn't no way of contenting her, she was
so all-fired pernicketty. There was another ship
in the harbor near us, and the captain was a sort
of a kind of a cousin of mother's, and so I
shipped with him and we come straight home
from Genoa to Portsmouth. And when I wanted
to enlist they wouldn't have me, saying I was too
young, which was all foolishness. So I went for
a drummer-boy, and I was in the Army of the
Potomac from Gettysburg to Appomattox."

"You were only a boy even when the war was over," I commented.

"Well, I was seventeen, and I felt old enough to be seventy," he returned, as a smile wrinkled his lean features. "At any rate, I was old enough to get married the year after Lee surrendered, and my daughter was born the year after that— she'd be nearly thirty now if she was living to-day."

"Did you stay in one of the bands of the regulars after the war?" I asked, wondering how the sailor-lad who had become a drummer-boy had finally developed into a solo orchestra.

"No," he answered. "Not but what I did think of it some. But after being at sea so long and in the army, camping here and there and always moving on, I was restless, and I didn't want to settle down nowhere for long. So I went into the show business. I'd always been fond of music, and I could play on 'most anything, from a fine-tooth comb to a church-organ with all the stops you please. So I went out with the side-show of a circus, playing on the tumbleronicon."

"The tumbleronicon?" I repeated, in doubt.

"It's a tray with a lot of wineglasses on it and goblets and tumblers, partly filled with water, you know, so as to give different notes. Why, I've had one tumbleronicon of seven octaves that I used to play the 'Anvil Chorus' on, and always got a double encore for it. I believe it's what they used to call the 'musical glasses'—but tumbleronicon is what it's called now in the profession."

I admitted that I had heard of the musical glasses.

"It was while I was playing the tumbleronicon in that side-show that I met the lady I married," he went on. "She was a Circassian girl then. Most Circassian girls are Irish, you know, but she wasn't. She was from the White Mountains. Well, I made up to her from the start, and when the circus went into winter-quarters we had a lot of money saved up and we got married. My wife hadn't a bad ear for music, so that winter we worked up a double act, and in the spring we went on the road as Swiss Bell-ringers. We dressed up just as I had seen the I-talians dress in Naples."

Again I asked for an explanation.

"Oh, you must have seen that act?" he urged, "though it has somehow gone out of style lately. It's to have a fine set of bells, three or four octaves, laying out on a table before you, and then you play tunes on them, just as you do on the tumbleronicon. There's some tunes go better on the bells than on anything else—'Yankee Doodle' and 'Pop Goes the Weasel.' It's quick tunes like them that folks like to have you pick out on the bells. Why, Mrs. Briggs and I used to do a patriotic medley, ending up with 'Rally Round the Flag,' that just made the soldiers' widows cry. If we could only have gone on, we'd

have been sure of our everlasting fortunes. But
Mrs. Briggs went and lost her health after our
daughter was born the next summer. We kept
thinking all the time she'd get better soon, and
so I took an engagement here in New York, at
Barnum's old museum in Broadway, to play the
drum in the orchestra. You remember Barnum's old museum, don't you ?"

I was able to say that I did remember Barnum's old museum in Broadway.

" I didn't really like it there : for the animals
were smelly, you know, and the work was very
confining, what with two and three performances
a day. But I had to stay here in New York somehow, for my wife wa'n't able to get away. The
long and short of it is, she was sick a-bed nigh
on to thirty years—not suffering really all the
time, of course, but puny and ailing, and getting no comfort from her food. There was times
I thought she never would get well or anything. But two years ago she up and died suddenly, just when I'd most got used to her being
sick. Women's dreadful uncertain, ain't they ?"

I had to confess that the course of the female
of our species was more or less incalculable.

" My daughter, she died the year before her
mother : and she'd never been sick a day in her
life—took after me, she did," Professor Briggs
went on. "She and her husband used to do
Yankee Girl and Irish Boy duets in the vaude-
villes, as they call them now."

I remarked that variety show, the old name for entertainments of that type, seemed to me more appropriate.

"That's what I think myself," he returned, "and that's what I'm always telling them. But they say vaudeville is more up to date—and that's what they want now, everything up to date. Now I think there's lots of the old-fashioned things that's heaps better than some of these new-fangled things they're so proud of. Take a three-ringed circus, for instance—what good is a three-ringed circus to anybody, except the boss of it ? The public has only two eyes apiece, that's all—and even a man who squints can't see more than two rings at once, can he ? And three rings don't give a real artist a show: they discourage him by distracting folk's attention away from him. How is he to do his best if he can't never be certain sure that the public is looking at him?"

Here again I was able to express my full agreement with the professor.

" I'd never do in a three-ring show, no matter what they was to give me," he continued. " And I've got an act nearly ready now that there's lots of these shows will be wanting just as soon as they hear of it. I "—here he interrupted himself and looked up and down the street, as though to make sure that there were no concealed listeners lying in wait to overhear what he was about to say—" I don't mind telling you about it, if you'd like to know."

I declared that I was much interested, and that I desired above all things to learn all about this new act of his.

"Well," he began, "I think I told you awhile ago that my granddaughter's all the family I got left now? She's nearly eight years old, and as cunning a little thing as ever you see anywhere—and healthy, too, like her mother. She favors me, just as her mother did. And she takes to music naturally—can't keep her hands off my instruments when I put them down—plays 'Jerusalem the Golden' on the pipes now so it would draw tears from a graven image. And she sings too—just as if she couldn't help it. She's a voice like an angel—oh, she'll be a primy donny one of these days. And it was her singing gave me the idea of this new act of mine. It's *Uncle Tom's Cabin* arranged just for her and me. I do Uncle Tom and play the fiddle, and she doubles Little Eva and Topsy with a lightning change. As Little Eva, of course, she'll sing a hymn—'Wait Till the Clouds Roll By,' or the 'Sweet By-and-By,' or something of that sort; and as Topsy she'll do a banjo solo first, and then for the encore she'll do a song and dance, while I play the fiddle for her. It's a great scheme, isn't it? It's bound to be a go!"

I expressed the opinion that it seemed to me a most attractive suggestion.

"But I've made up my mind," he went on, "not to bring her out at all until I can get the right opening. I don't care about terms first off, because when we make our hit we can get our own terms quick enough. But there's everything in opening right. So I shall wait till fall, or maybe even till New Year's, before I begin to worry about it. And in the meantime my own act in the street goes. The Solo Orchestra is safe for pretty good money all summer. You didn't hear me the other evening, and I'm sorry —but there's no doubt it's a go. I don't suppose it's as legitimate as the tumbleronicon, maybe, or as the Swiss bells—I don't know for sure. But it isn't bad, either ; and in summer, wherever there's children around, it's a certain winner. Sometimes when I do the ' Turkish Patrol,' or things like that, there's a hundred or more all round me."

" From the way the little ones looked at me the other evening, when I asked you to move on," I said, " it was obvious enough that they were very anxious to hear you. And I regret that I was forced to deprive myself also of the pleasure."

He rose to his feet slowly, his loose-jointed frame seeming to unfold itself link by link.

" I tell you what I'll do," he responded, cordially ; " isn't your lady getting better ?"

I was able to say that our invalid was improving steadily.

" Well, then," he suggested, " what do you say to my coming round here some evening next week ? I'll give a concert for her and you, and any of your friends you like to invite ? And you can tell her there isn't any of the new songs or waltzes or marches or selections from operas she wants I can't do. She's only got to give it a name and the Solo Orchestra will play it."

Of course I accepted this proffered entertainment ; and with that Professor Briggs took his leave, bidding me farewell with a slightly conscious air as though he were accustomed to have the eyes of a multitude centred upon him.

And one evening, in the middle of the week, the Solo Orchestra appeared on the sidewalk in front of our house and gave a concert for our special benefit.

Our invalid had so far regained her strength that she was able to sit at the window to watch the performance of Professor Briggs. But her attention was soon distracted from the Solo Orchestra itself to the swarm of children which encompassed him about, and which took the sharpest interest in his strange performance.

" Just look at that lovely little girl on the stoop opposite, sitting all alone by herself, as though she didn't know any of the others," cried our convalescent. "She's the most elfinlike little beauty I've ever seen. And she is as *blasée* about this Solo Orchestra of yours as though it was *Tannhäuser* we were listening to, and she was the owner of a box at the Metropolitan."

When the concert came to an end at last, as

the brief twilight was waning, when the Solo
Orchestra had played the "Anvil Chorus" as a
final encore after the "Turkish Patrol," when
Professor Theophilus Briggs, after taking up the
collection himself, had shaken hands with me
when I went down to convey to him our thanks,
when it was so plainly evident that the performance was over at last that even the children accepted the inevitable and began to scatter—then
the self-possessed little girl on the opposite side
of the way rose to her feet with dignity.   When
the tall musician, with the bells jingling in his
peaked hat, crossed the street, she took his hand
as though he belonged to her.   As he walked
away she trotted along by his side, smiling up
at him.

"I see now," I said : "that must be his granddaughter, the future impersonator of the great
dual character, Little Eva and Topsy."

(1896)

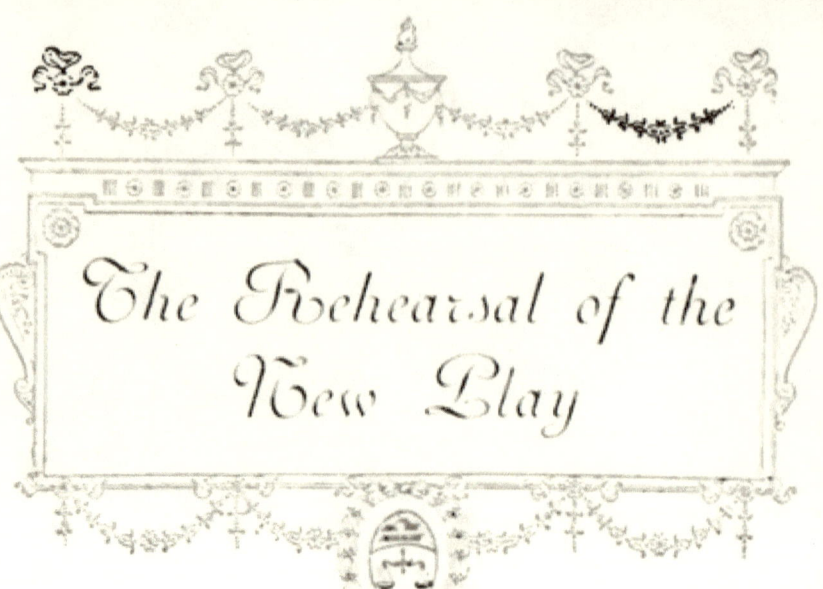

The Rehearsal of the New Play

HEN Wilson Carpenter came to the junction of the two great thoroughfares, he stood still for a moment and looked at his watch, not wishing to arrive at the rehearsal too early. He found that it was then almost eight o'clock, and he began at once to pick his way across the car-tracks that were here twisted in every direction. A cloud of steam swirled down as a train on the elevated railroad clattered along over his head ; the Cyclops eye of a cable-car glared at him as it came rushing down-town : from the steeple of a church on the corner, around which the mellow harvest-moon peered down on the noisy streets, there came the melodious call to the evening service : over the entrance to a variety show a block above a gaudy cluster of electric lights illuminated the posters which proclaimed for that evening a Grand Sacred Concert, at which Queenie Dougherty, the Irish Empress, would sing her new song, "He's an Illigant Man in a Scrap, My Boys." As the young dramatist sped along he noted that people were still straggling by twos and threes into the house of worship and into the place of entertainment : and he could not but contrast swiftly this Sunday

evening in a great city with the Sunday evenings
of his boyhood in the little village of his birth.

He wondered what his quiet parents would
think of him now were they alive, and did they
know that he was then going to the final rehearsal of a play of which he was half author.
It was not his first piece, for he had been lucky
enough the winter before to win a prize offered
by an enterprising newspaper for the best one-act
comedy ; but it was the first play of his to be produced at an important New York house.   When
he came to the closed but brilliantly lighted entrance of this theatre, he stood still again to read
with keen pleasure the three-sheet posters on
each side of the doorway.   These parti-colored
advertisements announced the first appearance
at that theatre of the young American actress,
Miss Daisy Fostelle, in a new American comedy,
" Touch and Go," written expressly for her by
Harry Brackett and Wilson Carpenter, and produced under the immediate direction of Z. Kilburn.

When the author of the new American comedy
had read this poster twice, he took out his watch
again and saw that it was just eight.   He threw
away his cigarette and walked swiftly around the
corner.   Entering a small door, he went down a
long, ill-lighted passage.   At the end of this was
a small square hall, which might almost be called
the landing-stage of a flight of stairs leading to
the dressing-rooms above and to the property-

room below. This hall was cut off from the stage by a large swinging-door.

As Carpenter entered the room this door swung open and a nervous young man rushed in. Catching sight of the dramatist, he checked his speed, held out his hand, and smiled wearily, saying, "That's you, is it? I'm so glad you've come!"

"The rehearsal hasn't begun, has it?" Carpenter asked, eagerly.

"Star isn't here yet," answered the actor, "and she's never in a hurry, you know. She takes her own time always, Daisy does. I know all her little tricks. I've told you already that I never would have accepted this engagement at all if I hadn't been out since January. I don't see myself in this part of yours. I'll do my best with it, of course, and it isn't such a bad part, maybe; but I don't see myself in it."

Carpenter tapped the other on the back heartily and cried: "Don't you be afraid, Dresser; you will be all right! Why, I shouldn't wonder if you made the hit of the whole piece!"

And with that he started to open the door that led to the stage.

But Dresser made a sudden appeal: "Don't go away just as I've found you. I've been wanting to see you all day. I've got to have your advice, and it's important."

"Well?" the dramatist responded.

"Well," repeated the young actor, "you know that bit of mine in the third act, where I have the scene with Jimmy Stark ? He has to say to me, 'I think my wife's mind is breaking,' and I say, 'Are you afraid she is going to give you a piece of it ?' Now, how would you read that ?"

After the author had explained to the actor what seemed to him the obvious distribution of the emphasis in this speech, he was able to escape and at last to make his way upon the stage.

The scene of the first act of "Touch and Go" was set, and the stage itself was brilliantly lighted, while the auditorium was in absolute darkness. It was at least a minute before Carpenter was able to discern the circle of the balcony, shrouded in the linen draperies that protected its velvet and its gilding from the dust. Here and there in the orchestra chairs were little knots of three or four persons, perhaps twenty or thirty in all. The proscenium boxes yawned blackly. Although it was a warm evening in the early fall, the house struck Carpenter as chill and forbidding. He peered into the darkness to discover the face he was longing to see again.

Two men were talking earnestly, seated at a table in the centre of the stage near the footlights. One of these was a short man, with grizzled hair and a masterful manner. This was Sherrington, the stage-manager who had been engaged to produce the play. The other was Harry Brackett, Carpenter's collaborator in its authorship.

Just as the new-comer had made out in the

dark house the group he was seeking and had bowed to the two ladies comprising it. Harry Brackett caught sight of him.

"Well, Will," he cried, "the Stellar Attraction is late, as usual—and we've got lots of work before us to-night, too. Sherrington isn't at all satisfied with the way they do either of the big scenes in the second act; and we've got to look out and keep them all up to their work if we want this to be anything more than a mere 'artistic success.'"

"'Artistic success!'" said Sherrington, emphatically; "why, there's money in this thing of yours—big money, too, if we can get all the laughs out of those two scenes of Daisy's in the second act. But it will take good work to get out all the laughs there ought to be, legitimately—and we've got to do it! Every laugh is worth a dollar and a half; that's what I say."

"The two scenes in the second act?" inquired Carpenter. "The one with Stark and the one with Miss Marvin, you mean?"

"The one with Marvin will be all right, I think," said the stage-manager.

"I'm not so sure of that," Harry Brackett interjected; "you insisted on her being engaged, Will, but she is very inexperienced, and I don't know how she'll get through that long scene."

"Miss Marvin is very clever," Carpenter declared, eager to defend the girl he was in love with; "and she will look the part to perfection!"

"Looking is all very well," Brackett responded, "but it is acting she will have to do in that scene in the second act."

"And she will do it too," asserted the stage-manager. "You see, she's got her mother here to-night, and there isn't a sharper old stager anywhere than Kate Shannon Loraine."

"That's so," Harry Brackett admitted; "I suppose Loraine can show her daughter how to get out of that scene all there is in it."

"Shannon 'll see the whole play to-night," said Sherrington, "and she'll be able to give Marvin lots of pointers to-morrow. The little girl will be all right; it's Daisy I'm more afraid of in that scene. It ought to be played high comedy, 'Lady Teazle,' way up in G—and high comedy isn't altogether in Daisy's line."

"That can't be helped now," Brackett replied; "and if the Stellar Attraction can't reach that scene it's the Stellar Attraction's own fault, isn't it? You remember, Will, how she kept telling us all the time we were writing the play that she wanted as high-toned a part as we could give her. We gave it to her, and now she's just got to stretch up to it, if she can."

"I am not afraid of that scene," Carpenter declared, "for I've always doubted whether she could really do high comedy, and that scene is written so that it will go almost as well if it's played broadly. You know there are two ways of doing Lady Teazle."

" There are no two ways about Daisy's being a great favorite." said the stage-manager. " She's accepted, and that's enough. After all. I don't suppose it matters much how she takes that scene : high or broad, the public will accept her. The part fits her like a glove, and all we've got to do is to keep everybody up to concert-pitch and get all the laughs we can. You took my advice and cut that talky scene in the third act. and now the whole act will go off like hot cakes —see if it don't. I tell you what it is. I'll teach you two boys how to write a real farce before I've done with you !"

Harry Brackett was standing almost behind Sherrington as the stage - manager made this speech. He winked at Carpenter.

" Yes," he said, a moment later, " I think it is a pretty good piece of the kind. and I hope it will fetch them. At any rate. I don't believe even our worst enemies will praise it for its ' literary merit.' "

Carpenter laughed a little bitterly. " No," he assented. " we've got it into shape now. and I doubt if anybody insults us by saying that ' Touch and Go ' is ' well written.' "

" Do you remember our joke while we were working on it last winter, Will ?" asked Harry Brackett. Then turning to Sherrington he explained : " We used to say that the managers wouldn't ' touch' it, so the people couldn't ' go.' "

" It's harder to touch the manager than it is

to make the public go," added Carpenter. "I believe that any fool can write a play, but that only a man of great genius ever succeeds in getting his play produced."

A handsome young woman with snapping black eyes walked on the stage briskly.

"Here's the Stellar Attraction at last," said Harry Brackett; "now we can get down to business."

"Am I late?" the handsome young woman asked, as she came forward. "Everybody waiting for me?"

"You are just twenty minutes late, my dear," said the stage-manager, looking at his watch, "and we are all waiting for you."

"That's all right, then," she replied, laughing lightly; "we've got all night before us, haven't we?"

The prompter clapped his hands and called out "First act!" Two clean-shaven men of indefinite age who had been sitting in the wings rose and came forward. Mr. Dresser joined them, and his manner suggested a certain increase of his ordinary nervous tension. A well-preserved elderly lady left her seat on one side of the aisles under the proscenium box and came through the door which led from the auditorium to the stage. She was followed by a slight, graceful girl, a blonde with clear gray eyes.

"Mrs. Castleman — Miss Marvin," said the prompter, seeing them: "now we are all ready."

And then the serious business of the rehearsal began. Mrs. Castleman came down to the centre of the stage and took up a newspaper and read the date of it aloud. and remarked that it was just five years since master and mistress had parted in anger, adding that neither of them had put foot inside the old house in all the five years. and yet it was not an hour from New York. Then one of the minor actors, an awkward young fellow. one of the two who had been standing in the wings, entered with a telegram, which he gave to Mrs. Castleman. She tore it open and read it aloud : the master would arrive early that evening. Then Miss Marvin. the girl with the clear blue eyes. came forward with an open letter in her hand and told Mrs. Castleman that the mistress of the house would be home again at last late that afternoon. And thus the rehearsal went on gravely. every one intent upon the business in hand. The speeches of the actors were interrupted now and then by the stage-manager. "Take the last scene over again." he might command, whereupon the performers would resume their places as before and begin again. "Don't cross till he takes the stage, my dear. And when he says. 'What is the meaning of this ?' don't be in a hurry. Wait. and then say your aside. 'Can he suspect ?' in a hoarse whisper. See ?"

Finally there was a jingle of sleigh-bells. and the orchestra. beginning faintly and slowly. soon

11

worked up to a swift *forte*, and then Miss Daisy
Fostelle made her first appearance through the
broad door at the back of the stage.   Finding
that she had taken everybody by surprise, she
smiled sweetly, and said, " You didn't expect
me, I see—but I hope you are all glad to see me
once more."

A thin, cadaverous man with a heavy, black
mustache here stepped forward to face the wife
he had not seen for five years. " We are all glad
to see you once more," he had to say, " very glad
indeed, and we are gladder still to see that you
seem to be in such excellent health and such
high spirits! The separation has not dimmed the
brightness of your eyes, nor—" Here the tall,
gaunt actor stopped and hesitated. " I don't
know what's the matter with that speech," he
said, impatiently, " but I can't get it into my
head.   I never had such tricky lines!"

The prompter gave him the word he needed,
and no one else paid any attention to this out-
break.

The two authors were seated at the table in the
centre of the footlights, and Harry Brackett
whispered to Carpenter: " Stark is getting the
big head, isn't he? The idea of a mere cuff-
shooter like that taking himself seriously!"

Then there followed an important scene in
which the wife gave her husband a witty and
vivacious account of all her doings during the
five years of their separation, ending with the

startling announcement that she had spent six weeks in South Dakota and had there procured a divorce from him! But there is no need to disclose here in detail the plot of "Touch and Go," as the new American comedy unfolded itself scene by scene. As the end of the act approached Sherrington pressed the actors to play more briskly so as to bring the curtain down swiftly on an unexpected but carefully prepared tableau.

When the act was over the stage manager had the final passages repeated twice, to make sure of its going smoothly at the first performance; and then the stage was cleared so that the scene might be set for the second act.

Carpenter watched the graceful, gray-eyed girl go back into the dim auditorium and take a seat beside her mother; and his heart thumped suddenly as he found himself wondering when he would dare to tell her that he loved her and to ask her to be his wife. Then he also left the stage and dropped into the chair behind mother and daughter.

"It was very good of you to come this evening, Mrs. Loraine," he began. "I feel as if having your daughter act in this play of mine will bring me luck somehow."

"The idea!" said Miss Marvin, smilingly.

"Mary had told me how clever the piece was," the elder actress responded, "but it is really better than she said. The dialogue is very brilliant at times, and the characters are excellently contrasted—and, what is more important, the whole thing will act! The parts carry the actors; they've got something to do which is worth while doing. It will go all right to-morrow night!"

"It's a beautiful piece," Mary Marvin declared, "and I think my part is just lovely!"

And before he could say anything in fit acknowledgment, Mrs. Loraine went on: "Yes, Mary's part is charming. And I think she will play it very well, too!"

"I'm sure of it!" he cried, unhesitatingly.

"I think there is more in it than I thought at first," said Mary's mother, "now I've seen the play, and I'll go over Mary's part with her to-night and show her what can be done with it. I'm waiting for that scene in the second act with Fostelle. I think that Mary ought to share the call after that. In fact, I'm not sure that she can't take the scene away from Fostelle."

"Oh, mother," the daughter broke in, "that would never do! I should get my two weeks' notice the next morning, shouldn't I? And I don't want to be out of an engagement just at the beginning of the season when all the companies are made up."

"Are you sure that the ghost will walk every week with this Fostelle company, if you strike bad business for a month or so?" asked Mrs. Loraine, with a suggestion of anxiety in her voice.

" I think Zeke Kilburn is all right," the dramatic author responded ; " he made a pile of money last year on that imported melodrama, the ' Doctor's Daughter ' ; and, besides, he has a backer."

Mrs. Loraine laughed gently, showing her beautifully regular teeth. She was still a handsome woman, with a fine figure and a crown of silver hair.

" A backer ?" she rejoined : " but who backs the backer ? I've heard your friend, Mr. Brackett, there, say that a jay and his money are soon parted."

Carpenter answered her earnestly. " I really think Kilburn is pretty solid, but I suppose that a great deal does depend on the way that the play draws. They've got open time here in New York, and if ' Touch and Go ' catches on they can stay here till Christmas. So it comes down to this, that if our piece is a go the ghost will walk regularly."

" I hope it will make a hit," Mrs. Loraine answered, " for your sake, too. You haven't sold it outright, have you ?"

" No, indeed," the young dramatist replied. " Harry Brackett is too old in the business for that. We've got a nightly royalty, with a percentage on the gross whenever it plays to more than four thousand dollars a week. We stand to make a lot of money—if it makes a hit. What do you think of its chances, Mrs. Loraine ?"

"The first act is all right," she responded. "That's the most I can say now. But come and ask me after I've seen the third act and I'll tell you what I think, and I believe I can then prophesy its fate pretty well."

By this time the scene of the second act had been set. It represented a stone summer-house on the top of a hill overlooking the Hudson just below West Point. It was picturesque in itself, and it was ingeniously arranged to provide opportunities for effective stage business.

Carpenter accompanied Miss Marvin back to the stage when the time drew nigh for the second act to begin.

As he was passing through the door between the auditorium and the stage, he found himself face to face with Dresser, who was fidgeting to and fro.

"Oh, Mr. Carpenter," he cried, "I'm so glad to see you! I want to ask your opinion about this. After all, you know, you wrote the play, and you ought to be able to decide. In my scene with Marvin in this act, am I really in love with her then, or ain't I? Sherrington says I am, but I think it's a great deal funnier if I'm not in love with her then—it helps to work up the last act better. Now what do you think? Sherrington insists that his way of playing it is more dramatic. Well, I don't say it ain't, but it isn't half as funny, is it?"

After Carpenter had given his opinion upon

this question, Dresser allowed him to escape. But he had not advanced ten yards before he was claimed by Mrs. Castleman.

"Mr. Carpenter," the elderly actress began, in her usual haughtily dignified manner, "how do you think I ought to dress this part in the first act? She's a house-keeper, isn't she? So I suppose I ought to wear an apron."

The young dramatist expressed his belief that perhaps an apron would be a proper thing for the house-keeper to wear in the first act.

"But not a cap, I hope?" urged Mrs. Castleman.

Carpenter doubted if a cap would be necessary.

"Thank you," said Mrs. Castleman. "You see, I have always hitherto been associated with the legitimate, and I really don't quite know what to do with this sort of thing." Then she suddenly paused, only to break out again impetuously: "Oh, I beg your pardon, Mr. Carpenter, really I did not mean to imply that this charming play of yours is not legitimate—"

The dramatic author laughed. "You needn't apologize," he declared: "I'm inclined to think that 'Touch and Go' is so illegitimate now that its own parents can't recognize it!"

At last the rehearsal of the second act began, the two authors sitting at the little table with the stage-manager.

Sherrington consulted them once or twice in regard to the omission of a line here and there.

"Cut it down to the bone when you can—

that's what I say," he explained; "what you cut out can't make people yawn."

But once he stopped the rehearsal to suggest that a speech be written in. "You've got to make that complication mighty clear," he declared, "and this is the place to do it, I think. If you want them to understand that Dresser here is going to mistake Marvin for Fostelle in the next scene, you had better give him another line now to lead up to it."

The two authors consulted hastily, and Carpenter, drawing out a note-book and a pencil, hurriedly wrote a sentence, which he showed to Brackett.

"That 'll do it," said Sherrington; and he read it aloud to Dresser, who borrowed Carpenter's pencil and wrote in the line on the manuscript of his part, wondering aloud whether he should ever remember it on the first night.

A few minutes later Sherrington again interrupted the actors to insist that the sunset effect should be adjusted carefully to accompany the spoken dialogue.

"I want a soft, rosy tinge on Fostelle in this scene," he explained.

"Quite right," laughed the black-eyed star; "that ought to be becoming to my style of beauty."

"And I want it to contrast with the blue moonlight in the scene with Marvin," said the stage-manager.

"Quite right again," Miss Daisy Fostelle commented. "I'll take the centre of the stage, and you will order calciums for one!"

"We had better go back to your entrance, I think," Sherrington decided, "and take the whole scene over."

The actors and actresses obediently resumed the positions they had occupied when Miss Daisy Fostelle made her first appearance in that act. The cue for her entrance was given, and she came forward with a burst of artificial laughter.

"That laugh was very good," Sherrington declared—"better than it was last time; but you must make it as hollow as you can. Remember the situation: your best young man has gone back on you and you are trying to keep a stiff upper-lip—but your heart is breaking all the same. See?"

The star repeated the laugh, and it was more obviously artificial.

"That's it, my dear," said the stage-manager. "Now keep it up till you cross, and then drop into that chair there, and then you let the laugh die away into a sob."

The star went back to the rustic gate by which she had entered, laughed again, and came forward; then she crossed the stage, sank upon a seat, and choked with a sob.

Carpenter stepped forward and whispered into Sherrington's ear, whereupon Miss Fostelle sat upright instantly and very suspiciously asked,

"What's that? I'd rather have you say it out loud than whisper it!"

The young dramatist explained at once.

"I was only suggesting to Sherrington that perhaps it would be better if that seat were turned a little so that you were not so sideways: then the audience would get a full view of your face here."

"It would be a pity to deprive them of that, I'll admit," said the mollified actress, as she and the stage-manager slightly turned the rustic chair.

Then she dropped into the seat and repeated her sob.

Miss Marvin stepped upon the stage, and remarked to space, "What a lovely evening, and how glorious the sunset!" Then she stood silently watching.

Miss Daisy Fostelle sobbed again, and, in tones heavy-laden with tears, she said, "What have I to live for now?" Looking back at the other actress she remarked, in her ordinary voice, "You will give me time to pick myself up here, won't you?" Then she went on, in the former tear-stained accents, "What have I left to live for now? My heart is broken! My heart is broken!" Again she resumed her every-day tones to ask the stage-manager: "Is that all right? Am I far enough around now?"

Thus they came to perhaps the most important scene of the play—that between the Stellar Attraction (as Brackett liked to call her) and the girl Carpenter was in love with. Both actresses were well fitted to the characters they had to perform. Carpenter, who had no liking for Daisy Fostelle, was a little surprised at the judgment and skill with which she carried off the *bravura* passages of her part ; and he was not a little charmed with the delicate force the gentle Mary Marvin revealed in the contrasting character.

And so the rehearsal proceeded laboriously, Sherrington directing it autocratically, ordering certain scenes to be played more rapidly and seeing that others were taken more slowly, so that the spectators might have time to understand the situation. Now and then either Carpenter or Brackett made a suggestion or a criticism, but both yielded to Sherrington, if he was insistent. The stage-manager kept the whole company of actors up to their work, and imposed on them his understanding of that work, much as the conductor of an orchestra leads his musicians at the performance of a symphony.

When the whole act had been rehearsed, and the final scene was repeated three or four times until it ran like well-oiled clockwork, the stage was cleared so that the scenery of the third act might be set.

Sherrington accompanied Miss Marvin through the door behind the proscenium box into the dark auditorium.

"You will play that scene very well," he said, "but you've got to have confidence."

"It is a beautiful part, isn't it?" she responded, with enthusiasm. "I never had a part I could enjoy playing so much."

Carpenter was about to leave the stage to tell Mary what a delight it was to him to hear her speak the words he had written, when his collaborator tapped him on the shoulder. As he turned Harry Brackett whispered in his ear:

"Look out for the Stellar Attraction. I'm afraid she has just dropped on Marvin's part. If she once suspects that the little girl may get that scene away from her, she can make herself mightily disagreeable all round. I guess we had better go up and tell her she is a greater actress than Charlotte Cushman."

Carpenter laughingly answered: "Take care she doesn't drop on you! It would be worse if she thought you were guying her."

"There's no danger of that," Harry Brackett returned. "That Stellar Attraction of ours is a boa-constrictor for flattery—there isn't anything she won't swallow."

The two dramatic authors found Miss Daisy Fostelle standing in the wings and discussing with Dresser the personal peculiarities of another member of the dramatic profession.

As Carpenter and Brackett came up the actress was saying: "Why, she had the check actually to tell me I was more amusing off the stage than

on—the cat! But I got even with her. I told
her I was sorry I couldn't return the compliment, for she was even less amusing on the
stage than off!"

The two dramatists joined in the laugh, and
then Harry Brackett began.

"Is it your hated rival you are having fun
with?" he asked. "Well, if she comes to see
you in this play to-morrow they'll have to put
a waterproof carpet into the private box, for
she will weep bitter tears of despair while she's
watching you in this second act of ours."

Miss Daisy Fostelle snapped her big black eyes
at him and smiled with pleasure.

"Yes," she admitted. "I don't believe she
will really enjoy that scene—and yet she'll have
to give me a hand at the end of the act."

"She'll go through the motions, perhaps,"
Brackett returned, "but she won't burst a hole
in her gloves." Then he slyly nudged his collaborator.

"The fact is," began Carpenter, thus admon-
ished, "I was just going to tell Harry Brackett
here that maybe we have made a mistake in writing you a high-comedy part like this—"

The actress flashed a suspicious glance at him,
but he went on as if unconscious of this.

"We can see now," he continued, "that you
are going to play this part so well that you will
make a great hit in it, and then the critics will
all be after you to play Lady Teazle and Rosalind.

They'll tell you that you are only wasting your talents in modern plays and that you ought to devote yourself to the legitimate."

The suspicion faded from Miss Daisy Fostelle's face and the smile of pleasure reappeared.

"That's so," Harry Brackett declared. "You will make such a hit in this part, I'm afraid, that Sheridan and Shakespeare will be good enough for you next season. Now that would be taking the bread out of our mouths!"

The actress laughed easily. "I don't think you would starve," she returned; "and I might, maybe—if I took to the legitimate. Not that it would be my first attempt, either, for I played Ariel in the 'Tempest' when I was a mere child. And it wasn't easy, I can tell you. Ariel's a real hard part, I think; there's a certain swing to the words, too, and you can't make up a line of your own if you get stuck, as I could in this piece of yours."

"No," Brackett confessed, solemnly, "the dialogue of 'Touch and Go' is not as rhythmic as the dialogue of the 'Tempest.'"

"And I've played François in 'Richelieu,' too," continued Miss Fostelle. "But I don't think I really like any of those Shakespearian parts."

"No," Brackett confessed again, with fearless gravity. "François is not one of Shakespeare's best parts. It wasn't worthy of you, no matter how inexperienced you were. But Rosalind, now, as Carpenter suggests, and Beatrice—"

Carpenter here guessed from Dresser's spasmodic manner that the actor was about to intervene in the conversation, and not knowing what might be the result, the younger of the dramatists dropped out of the group and managed to draw Dresser away with him.

After they had exchanged a few words Carpenter looked into the auditorium to discover where Mary Marvin might be. He saw that she was by the side of her mother, and that Mrs. Loraine and Sherrington were still engaged in an earnest conversation. He made a movement as if to leave Dresser, whereupon the comedian begged him for a moment's interview.

"It's about that speech of mine in the third act that I want to make a suggestion," said the actor. "It's a very good speech, too, and I think I can get three laughs out of it, easy. You know the speech. I mean the one about the three old maids: 'There were three old maids in our town; one was as plain as a pikestaff, and the other was as homely as a hedge fence, and the third was as ugly as sin : and whenever they all three walked out together every clock in the place stopped short. Their parents had christened them Faith and Hope and Charity ; but the boys always called them Battle and Murder and Sudden Death.' Now, don't you think it would help to ring out the point more if the orchestra was to play 'Grandfather's Clock' very gently just as I say that 'every clock in the place stopped short'? What do you think? That's my own idea!"

The dramatist said nothing for a second or two, and then told the actor to consult the stage-manager, who was just returning to begin the rehearsal of the third act.

The new scene had been set swiftly and the furniture was already in place. The first of the actors to enter was the cadaverous and irritable Stark. He began glibly enough, but soon hesitated for a word, and then broke out impatiently, regardless of the presence of the two authors: "Oh, I can't get that line into my head! And I don't know what it means, either! How can you expect a man to speak such rubbish?"

As before, nobody paid any attention to this petulance, and the actor went on with his part without further comment.

Dresser then entered, and the two men proceeded to misunderstand each other in the most elaborate fashion. The character which Stark represented had reason to believe that the character that Dresser represented was the uncle of the character that Daisy Fostelle represented and was also a soldier. In like manner Dresser had reason to believe that Stark was the lady's uncle and also a sailor. They addressed each other, therefore, in sailor talk and in soldier talk; and the fun waxed fast and furious. At the height of the misunderstanding Daisy Fostelle entered unexpectedly and found herself instant-

ly immeshed in the humorous complication, with
no possibility of plausible explanation.

Once the stage-manager reminded Dresser that
he had omitted a phrase. "You left out 'Confound it, man!'" he said.

"I know it," the actor explained, "but I
wanted to save it to use in my next speech. It
goes better there—you see if it does not."

And Sherrington decided that "Confound it,
man!" was more effective in the later speech; so
the transposition was authorized, to Dresser's satisfaction.

The stage-manager had this important scene
of mutual misunderstanding between Stark and
Dresser and Daisy Fostelle repeated twice, until
every word fell glibly and every gesture seemed
automatic. And so the rehearsal went to the
end, Sherrington applying the finishing touches,
and seeming at last to be fairly well satisfied with
the result of his labors.

The final lines of the comedy were, of course,
to be delivered by the star: but when the cue was
given to her Miss Fostelle simply said "Tag!"
everybody being aware that it is very unlucky to
speak the last speech of a play at a rehearsal—as
unlucky as it is to put up an umbrella on the
stage, or to quote from "Macbeth."

"That will do," said the stage-manager; "I
think it will be all right to-morrow night."

And with that the rehearsal concluded and
the company began to disperse.

12

"I hope it is all right," Harry Brackett remarked to Carpenter, "and I think it is. But I
shall have a great deal more confidence after the
man in the box-office shakes hands with me cordially, say, next Wednesday or Thursday, and in-
quires about my health. He'll know by that time
whether we've got a good thing or not!"

Carpenter helped Miss Marvin to put on her
light cape. Then, after her mother had joined
them, they said good-night to the others and left
the theatre together.

When they came out into the warm night the
street was quieter than it had been when Carpenter entered the theatre. There were fewer cable-
cars passing the door, and the trains on the elevated road in the avenue were now infrequent.
The lights had been turned out in front of the
variety show across the way, and evidently the
grand sacred concert was over. The moon had
sunk, and before they had gone a block the bell
of the church tolled the hour of midnight.

The young man who was walking by the side
of Mrs. Loraine broke the silence at last.

"Well," he asked, "what do you think of the
play now?"

"I think it is a good piece of its kind," the
elder actress answered—"a very good piece of its
kind; and it is well staged; and it will be well
acted, too. Sherrington knows how to get his
best work out of everybody. Yes, it will be a
success."

"Is it good for three months here now?" the young author asked, "and for the rest of the season on the road?"

"Oh yes, indeed," replied Mrs. Loraine: "yes, indeed. It's safe for a hundred nights here at least!"

They paused at the corner to wait for a cable-car, and Sherrington joined them.

This gave Carpenter a chance to lead the daughter away from the mother half a dozen steps.

"I'm so glad mother thinks the play will go," the girl began. "And mother is a very good judge, too. You ought to make a lot out of it."

The young dramatist felt that he had his chance at last.

"I've wanted to make money mainly for one reason," he returned; "I wanted to ask you to take half of it."

"Half of it?" she echoed, as though she did not understand.

"Oh, well—all of it," he responded, swiftly: "and me with it."

"Mr. Carpenter!" she cried, and her blushes made her look even lovelier than before.

"Won't you marry me?" he asked, ardently.

"Oh, I suppose I've got to say yes," she answered, "or else you'll go down on your knees here in the street!"

(1896)

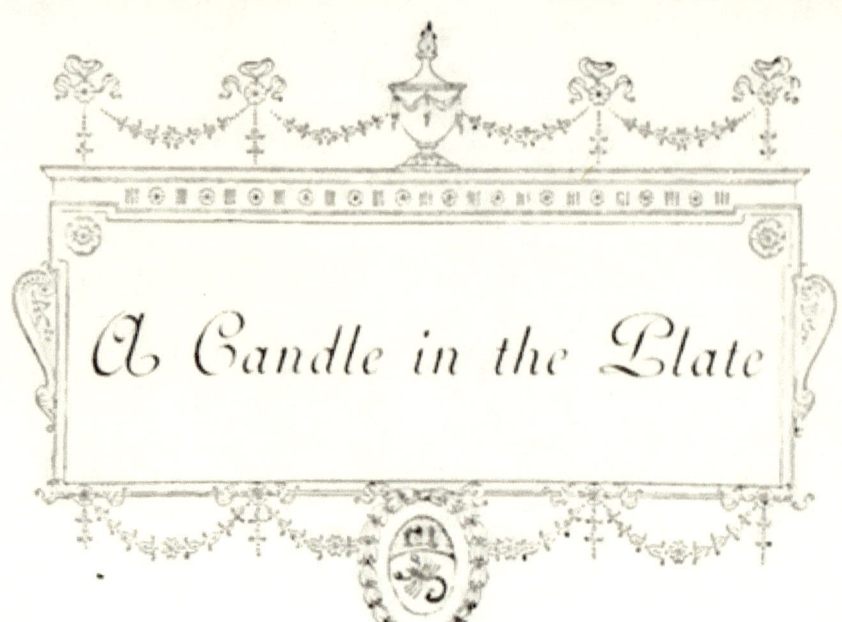

A Candle in the Plate

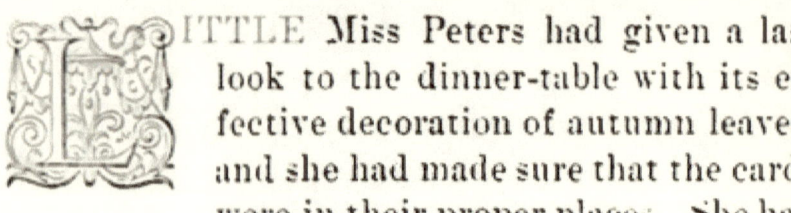ITTLE Miss Peters had given a last look to the dinner-table with its effective decoration of autumn leaves, and she had made sure that the cards were in their proper places. She had glanced at herself in the mirror of the music-room as she passed through, and she had smiled to see the little spot of color burning in her cheek. She had taken her place modestly behind her employer, the portly hostess, and she had seen the guests arrive one by one. She had remarked the cheerful eagerness of the young Irishman for whose sake the company had gathered, and she had frankly admired his good looks. Now she was sitting silently in her seat at the table, and she was wondering what the stranger would think of them all.

It would not be quite fair to the worthy widow to say that Mrs. Canton's dinners were always ponderous: but it might be admitted that, although the cooking was ever excellent and the guests were selected from the innermost circle of Society, the bill of fare was monotonous and the conversation often lacked variety. That evening, however, there were several present who had not before been honored with invitations to dine in that exclusive mansion. Few people of fashion were back in town so early in October, and it had not been easy for Mrs. Canton to make up her complement of guests when she found that she had suddenly to honor a letter of introduction Lord Mannington had given to the Honorable Gilbert Barry, brother of Lord Punchestown. She had heard that the handsome Irishman had been a great success at Lenox, and that all the girls were wild about him. In Mannington's letter she was informed that the young man went in for slumming and all that sort of thing, and that he had been living in Toynbee Hall; she was besought, therefore, to make him acquainted with the people in New York most interested in the elevation of the lower classes.

This sentence of Lord Mannington's letter it was that had caused Mrs. Canton to invite Rupert de Ruyter, the novelist, for she happened to have read one of his stories about the wretched creatures living down in the Italian quarter, and she was sure he would be able to tell Mr. Barry all that the young Irishman might want to know about the slums of New York. She had been fortunate enough to get the Jimmy Suydams, too; and she knew that Mrs. Jimmy took such an interest in the poor, acting as patroness so often, and all that. Then when little Miss Peters had come in to write the invitations and to balance the check-book and to answer the accumulated notes, Mrs. Canton, having gone over the

list, looked at the pretty young secretary for a
minute without speaking, and then said, " It
won't be easy to get just the people one wants.
Why shouldn't you come, Miss Peters? You
belong to one of those things, you know, what
do you call them—Working Girls' Clubs—don't
you?"

" I'm a working girl myself, am I not?" Miss
Peters answered. " And I reckon I'm very glad
I've gotten the work to do."

" Then you can tell him anything Mr. de
Ruyter doesn't know about these sort of people.
How absurd for the younger brother of a peer to
bother himself about such things over here, isn't
it?" Mrs. Canton had returned. " Then that's
settled."

Although the Southern girl had not relished
the way the invitation had been proffered, she
had not declined it, glad to get a glimpse again
of the life of luxury to which she had been a
stranger since she had been earning her own
living: and thus it was that she was sitting silently in her seat at the dinner-table that evening in October, with Gilbert Barry and Rupert
de Ruyter opposite to her. She did not seem to
notice how the young Irishman glanced across
the table at her more than once with obvious
admiration, or how he tried to lure her into the
conversation.

It irritated Miss Peters to have Rupert de Ruyter monopolize the talk. His rather rasping voice

sawed her nerves, and she detested the way he
thrust forward his square chin. She listened
while he chattered along. not boasting exactly,
yet managing to convey the impression that he
knew more than any one else. Now and again he
did bring forth a picturesque fact. for which he
had the kodak eye of a reporter. He had the
happy - go - lucky facility of the newspaper man,
and he rattled away with more than one absurd
misapprehension of the reality. until he reminded her of a singer with a fine voice but unable to
avoid false notes.

"I don't pretend to know New York inside-
out and upsidedown." he was saying ; "but it
is a most fascinating study. this polyglot city of
ours. and the more you push your investigations
the more likely you are to make surprising dis-
coveries. You know we have an Italian quarter
here ?"

This was addressed, perhaps, to the British
guest. but it was Mrs. Jimmy Suydam who answered it.

"Of course we do," she said ; "haven't we all
read that thrilling story you wrote about it ?—
the story with the startling title—*A Vision of
Black Despair.*"

The author flushed with pride that so handsome a woman and so exclusive a leader of Society should thus praise one of his writings.

Mr. Jimmy Suydam leaned over to Mrs. Canton, at whose left he was sitting. and said, "I

don't see how my wife does it. do you? She keeps up with everything. you know—reads all the books—and all that."

"I didn't mean to remind you of that little thing of mine," continued De Ruyter. with a self-satisfied air that made little Miss Peters feel as though she would like to stick a pin in him. "That's neither here nor there, though I spent two days down in the Italian quarter getting up the local color for it. But what you didn't know, any of you. I am certain, is that part of the soil of this city was imported from Italy."

"Really, now." commented the British guest. "that is very interesting. indeed. It would be from a religious motive. I suppose—just as some of the mediæval cemeteries had earth brought from the Holy Land?"

"That would be a more romantic reason, no doubt." the story-teller explained. "But the real one is very prosaic, I fear. The Italian soil here in New York was brought over as ballast by the ships that were going to take back our bread-stuffs. There is lot after lot upon the Harlem that has been filled in with this ballast—stones mostly. but some of it is earth."

"Genoa the superb providing a foundation for imperial New York," said the young Irishman, with a little flourish—and Miss Peters guessed that De Ruyter made a mental note of the figure for future elaboration. "And has New York a volcano under the city like Naples, now?—like

every great town in Europe for the matter of
that. Have you a seething mass of want and
misery and discontent, such as boiled over in
Paris under the Commune? That's what I'm
wanting to find out."

"We have a devil's cauldron of our own, if
that's what you mean," responded De Ruyter;
"and we have people from every corner of the
globe here now helping to keep the pot a-boiling.
We have Russian Jews by the thousand, living
just as they did in the Pale. We have Chinese
enough to support a Chinese theatre. We have
so many Syrians now that they are pre-empting
certain blocks for themselves. We have Irish
peasants so timid and suspicious that they won't
go to the hospital when they are almost dying,
because they believe the doctors keep a Black
Bottle to be administered to troublesome pa-
tients."

"I should think they would be ever so much
more comfortable in a roomy hospital than in
their stuffy little tenement-house rooms," said
Mrs. Jimmy; "and they can't get decent nursing
in their own homes, can they?"

"The poor are a most unreasonable lot—and
ungrateful, too," added Mr. Suydam; "that's
what I think."

"They are not so badly off in their tenement-
houses as you might think," explained De Ruyter.
"They help each other with the children when
there's sickness."

"The universal freemasonry of motherhood," commented Gilbert Barry; and again Miss Peters suspected the story-teller of making a mental record of the phrase.

"They are impossible to understand," De Ruyter declared.

"Why?" asked Miss Peters, suddenly, across the table, to the surprise of everybody. The young Irishman smiled encouragingly, as though he had been regretting that this pretty girl refused to talk.

"Why are they impossible to understand?" repeated the American story-teller. "I don't know, I'm sure. They are conundrums, all of them, and I am ready to give them up."

"Isn't it because you persist in approaching them as though they were strange, wild beasts?" the young woman went on. "You speak of them just as if they were different from us. But they are not, are they? They have their feelings just like we have: they fall in love and they get married and they quarrel and they die, just like we do. There is not more crime in the tenement-houses than there is in the rest of the city—not if you remember how many more people live in the tenement-houses. There isn't less joy there, or less sorrow either. There is quite as much happiness, I reckon, and a good deal more fun. They are not the lower animals: and it just makes me mad all over when I hear them spoken of in that way. They are human beings, after all—and if you can't understand them it's because you're not ready to go to them as your equals."

"That's what I say," the Irishman agreed; "we must approach them on the plane of human sympathy—that's the only way to get them to open their hearts."

"Why should we expect them to open their hearts to us?" Miss Peters continued. "We don't open ours to strangers, do we?"

"That's quite true," admitted Barry. "Sometimes I wonder if it isn't impertinent we are when we thrust ourselves into a poor man's room. I doubt we should like him to thrust himself into ours."

"I think that is a most amusing suggestion of yours," Mrs. Jimmy declared. "I shall look forward with delight to the day when the Five Points send missionaries up to Fifth Avenue."

"What an absurd idea!" cried Mrs. Canton, in disgust.

"Come now," the Irishman returned, "I deny that the suggestion is mine; but it is not so absurd—really, it isn't. There's lots of things they can teach us. I don't know but what we have more to learn from them than they have from us—really I don't. Christianity, now—practical Christianity—'inasmuch as ye did it to one of the least of these,' and all that sort of thing—well, there's more of that among the poor than there is among the rich, I'm thinking."

"If you want to pick up picturesque bits of low life in New York," broke in De Ruyter, "you must get a chance to see a candle in the plate."

"A candle in the plate?" echoed Barry. "I've never heard of it."

"It sounds like the title of a tale of superstition transplanted from Europe and surviving here in America," said Mrs. Jimmy.

"It's not a superstition, it's only a custom," De Ruyter explained: "and whether it's a transplanted survival or not I can't say. You see I've never seen the thing myself, but I've been told about it. I hear that down in the tenement-house region, when a family can't pay the rent and the landlord puts their scant furniture out on the sidewalk, and they don't know where to lay their heads that night, then one of the neighbors takes a candle and lights it and sticks it up on a plate, and takes his stand on the sidewalk: and this is a sign to everybody that there is a family in sore distress, and so the passers-by drop in a penny or two until there is enough to pay the arrears of rent and let the poor mother and children go back."

Mrs. Jimmy Suydam laughed a little bitterly. "That sort of thing may be possible on Cherry Hill," she said. "but it would never do on Murray Hill, would it? Just imagine how absurd a broken millionaire would look standing at a street corner with a little electric light on a silver sal-

ver, expecting the multi-millionaires going by to
drop in a check or two to pay his rent for him !"

"I thought I had a quaint little silhouette of
metropolitan life for you," De Ruyter responded, smiling back ; "but you spoil the picture if
you guy it like that."

"Very curious it is," said Barry—"very curious, indeed.   'How far a little candle throws its
beams.'   I don't think that the custom was ex-
ported from Ireland or from England—at least, I
do not recall anything analogous."

"I've heard an old Irishwoman complain that
the law was harder here on the tenant than it
was in the old country," Miss Peters asserted ;
and then she appended an imitation of the old
Irishwoman's speech : "'Sure, they'd boycott the
landlord there, that's what they'd do, or they'd
shoot the agent, maybe ; but here ye can't—
there's the police, bad cess to 'em !'"

"Have you ever seen the candle in the plate ?"
Barry asked her, across the table.

"Never," she answered.

"But you have heard of it ?" De Ruyter inquired.

"Never before to-night," was her reply.

"You don't mean to say you don't believe
that there is any such custom ?" Mrs. Jimmy
asked.   "Thus all our illusions are shattered
one by one."

"Of course, I don't know," the girl responded ; "I haven't been working down there very

long—only since last February. But it sounds like it was a fake, as we used to say in the newspaper office when I was a reporter."

Mrs. Jimmy Suydam had never met Miss Peters before, and now she examined the girl curiously, wondering what sort of being a woman was who had been a reporter and was now living among the poor, and who happened also to be dining at Mrs. Canton's.

The hostess was just then explaining to Mr. Suydam in a whisper that Miss Peters was a Southern girl of excellent family, who used to write those " Polly Perkins " articles for the *Dial* on Sunday, but who had given it up last winter, and now acted as her secretary.

" A fake ?" repeated the Irishman, gleefully ; " that's one of your Americanisms, isn't it ? I must remember that. A fake — what does it mean exactly ?"

" It means the thing that is not," De Ruyter explained, with a trace of acerbity in his voice. " Miss Peters disbelieves in the existence of the candle in the plate, and she was too polite to call my story a lie, so she said it was a fake."

" Oh, Mr. De Ruyter," was her retort, " and you used to be a newspaper man yourself once !"

" Your newspapers, now," Barry broke in, " I confess they puzzle me. They are so clever, you know, and so up-to-date, and all that ; but you never know what to believe in them, do you ? And then they do such dreadful things."

"I fear you will find few Americans prepared to defend our newspapers," said the story-teller, always a little ashamed that he had once been a reporter. "But what sort of a dreadful thing have you in mind just now?"

"Things quite inconceivable, you know," the Irishman explained; "a thing like this, for example. A year or two ago a man gave me a copy of one of your New York papers—the *Dial*, I think it was. I read it with great interest, as one would the writing of some strange tribe of savages, don't you know? It was so very extraordinary."

As the guest made this plain statement, little Miss Peters happened to catch the eye of the handsome Mrs. Jimmy Suydam, and they exchanged an imperceptible smile.

"What shocked me the most," Barry continued, "was a long article from some special commissioner, with headings in huge letters—"

"Scare-heads they call them," explained De Ruyter.

"Scare-heads?" repeated the Irishman. "That's the very name for them. Scare-heads —delicious! This article, then, had scare-heads galore, and it described how a suicide had been identified. It seems some poor girl of the working-class had got into trouble, and sooner than bring disgrace on her family she had jumped into the river here—Hudson's River, isn't it? She had carefully arranged so that there was no clew by which she could be traced. But she had not counted on the devilish ingenuity of the special commissioner, a woman, too—at least I suppose it was a woman, since the thing was signed ' Polly Perkins.' "

Mrs. Jimmy saw the blood rise in the cheeks of Miss Peters, until the little Southern girl was as red as any of the maple-leaves that decked the cloth between the two women. She noticed that Rupert De Ruyter was staring into his plate with ill-concealed embarrassment, and that Mrs. Canton seemed a little uneasy.

"It seems that the poor creature's body was sent to the Morgue," Barry continued, "and no one claimed it, so it was buried at the cost of the county. And there's where the diabolical cunning of this reporter was exercised. She guessed that the girl's family would want to see the body laid away in holy ground, and so she went to the burying. And she hit it, for there were two women there in deep black, the mother of the poor wretch and the sister, not afraid to show their bitter grief when they thought they were unknown and unwatched. The spy tracked them to their house and she found out their names, and she put the whole story in the paper ! I suppose it broke the mother's heart, and the sister's, to see the dead girl's shame brought home to her and to them when they thought it was buried in the grave with her body. I don't deny that the female detective showed a deal of skill : but what a pitiful thing! To risk breaking two loving hearts—and for what purpose?"

There was a moment's silence when the Irishman asked this unanswerable question. Then Miss Peters raised her head and looked him in the eye.

"That was what is called a 'beat.' No other paper had the news," she said; "and the reporter who wrote that story got a raise of five dollars a week."

"Faith, she deserved it," Barry returned. "It was blood-money she was taking, I'm thinking."

"That's what I think now," Miss Peters replied. "I wish I had thought so then. I wrote that article, and that is one reason why I am living down there among the poor, to try and make it up to them. Of course, I can't undo the wrong I did; but I mean to do my best."

Then there was another silence, broken by Mrs. Jimmy, who turned to Mrs. Canton and asked if she was going to take a box at the horse-show.

When the ladies left the dining-room Barry took the chair by the side of Suydam.

"What's the name of that pretty little girl?" he asked. "Peters, isn't it? I say, it was awfully plucky of her to tell us that she was 'Polly Perkins,' wasn't it, now? I like her; she's a trump! And that fair hair of hers is very fetching, isn't it?"

(1897)

Men and Women
and Horses

ERRYMOUNT MORTON walked briskly down Madison Avenue that warm November evening, when there was never a foretaste of winter in the intermittent breezes that blew gently across the city from river to river; and as he crossed the side streets one after another he saw the full moon in the east, low and large and mellow. On the brow of Murray Hill he checked his pace for a moment in frank enjoyment of the vista before him, differing in so many ways from the scenes which met his vision in the little college town of New England where he earned his living, and where he had spent the most of his life. The glow of the great town filled the air, and the roar of the city arose all about him. It seemed to him almost as though he could feel the heart of the metropolis throbbing before him. He caught himself wondering again whether he had not erred in accepting the professorship he had been so glad to get when he came back from Germany, and whether his life would not have been fuller and far richer had he come to New York, as once he thought of doing, and had he resolutely struck out for himself in the welter and chaos of the commercial capital of the country.

Down at the foot of the slope a cluster of electric lights spelled out the name of a trivial extravaganza then nearing its hundredth performance in the lovely Garden Theatre, and the avenue hereabouts had a strange, unnatural brilliance. High up in the pure dark blue the beautiful tower rose in air, its grace made visible by many lights of its own. The avenue was clogged with carriages, and the arcade before the theatre and under the tower was thick with men who carried under their arms folded card-board plans of the great amphitheatre, and who vociferously proffered tickets for the horse-show. So far remote from the current of fashion was Merrymount Morton that he had not been aware that the horse-show week was about to come to a glorious end. But he was familiar enough with New York to know that the horse-show was also an exhibition of men and women, and that the human entries were quite as important as the equine, and rather more interesting. He had never happened to be in the city at this season of the year; and although he had intended to spend the evening at the College Club, he seized the occasion to see a metropolitan spectacle which chanced to be novel to him.

From one of the shouting and insistent venders he bought a ticket, and he walked through the broad entrance-hall, the floor of which slanted upwards. He passed the door of a restaurant

on his right, and he glanced down a staircase
which led to the semi-subterranean stalls where
the horses were tethered. A pungent, acrid,
stable odor filled his nostrils. Then he found
himself inside the immense amphitheatre, under
the skeleton ribs of its roof picked out with long
lines of tiny electric bulbs. Morton had a first
impression of glittering hugeness, and a second
of restless bustle. From a gallery behind him
there came the blare and crash of a brass band
playing an Oriental march ; but even this did
not drown the buzz and murmur of many thousand voices. The vast building seemed to Morton to be filled with men and women, all of them
talking and many of them in motion. He found
himself swept along slowly in the dense crowd
that circled steadily around the high fence which
guarded the arena wherein the horses were ex-
hibited. This crowd was too compact for him
to approach the railing, and he could not discover for himself whether or not anything was
to be seen.

A thin line of more or less horsy fellows fringed
the fence, and seemed to be interested in what
was going on. The most of the men and women
who filled the broad promenade between the railing and the long tier of private boxes paid little
or no attention to the arena ; they gave themselves up to staring at the very gayly dressed
ladies in the boxes. It struck the New England
college professor that the most of those present

made no pretence of caring for the horses, as
though horses could be seen any day; while they
frankly devoted themselves to gazing at the people of fashion penned side by side in the boxes,
and not often placing themselves so plainly on
exhibition.   Some of those who were playing
their parts on this narrow and elevated stage
had the self-consciousness of the amateur, and
some had the ease that comes of long practice.
These latter looked as though they were accustomed to be stared at, as though they expected
it of right, as though they were there on purpose
to be seen.   They seemed to know one another;
and it struck Morton that they were apparently
all members of a secret fraternity of fashion,
with their own signs and passwords and their
own system of private grips; and they wholly
ignored the people who had not been initiated
and who were not members of their society.
They nodded and smiled brightly to belated
arrivals of their own set.   They kept up a con-
tinual chatter among themselves, the women
leaning across to talk to acquaintances in the
adjoining compartments, and the men paying
visits to the boxes of their friends.   Now and
again some one in a box would recognize some
one in the circling throng below; but for the
most part there was no communication between
the two classes.

    To Morton the spectacle had the attraction of
novelty; it was so novel, indeed, that he did not

EXPLANATIONS

quite know what to make of it. It disconcerted him not a little to see people, of position presumably, and obviously of wealth, willing thus to show themselves off, dressed, many of them, as though with special intent to attract attention. As a student of sociology, he found this inspection of Society — in the narrowest sense of the word — almost as instructive as it was interesting. At times the vulgarity of the whole thing shocked him, more especially once when he could not but hear the loud voices of one over-dressed group of women, who were discussing the characteristics of one " Willie."

" He's a wretched little beast !" cried one of these ladies.

" You mustn't say that," rejoined another, a tall woman with gray hair ; " you know he's my corespondent." And at this stroke of wit the rest of the party laughed repeatedly.

But few of those on exhibition were as common as the members of this group. Indeed, Morton was struck with the fact that the most of the men and women who were being stared out of countenance were apparently people of breeding, and he wondered that they were willing to place themselves in what seemed to him so false a position. Many of the girls, for example, who wore striking costumes and extravagant hats, were themselves refined in face and retiring in bearing ; they were stylish, no doubt, but they were well bred also. It seemed to Morton that style was perhaps the chief characteristic of these New York girls—style rather than beauty.

The average of good looks was high, and yet, as it happened, he was able to walk half around the huge building without seeing half a dozen women whom he was prepared to declare handsome. The girls appeared to be strong, healthy, lively, quick-witted, and charming, but rarely beautiful. They seemed to him, moreover, to be emphatically superior to the men who accompanied them, superior not only in looks, but in manners and intelligence.

Morton noted, to his surprise, that some of these men were quite as conscious of their clothes as any of the women were; and he caught also more than one remark showing that the appreciation of the women's clothes was not confined to the women themselves.

As he was nearing the Fourth Avenue end of the edifice he saw in a box just above him—for he found himself staring like the rest—a lady of striking beauty, with a look of sadness on her face, that gave place to a factitious smile when she spoke to one or another of the three or four young men who stood on the steps at the side of her chair. The face interested Morton, and it was recognized by two young men just behind him.

" Hello !" said one of them, " there's Mrs. Cyrus Poole. Smart gown, hasn't she ?"

" Always has," answered the other. " Best-groomed woman in New York."

"She is pretty well turned out generally, for a fact," the first speaker responded. "But Cyrus Poole's made money enough out of the widow and the orphan this summer to pay for all the gowns his wife can wear this winter, at any rate."

It was only when Merrymount Morton had threaded his way half around the horse-show that he first saw a horse there. As he came to the Fourth Avenue end the crowd before him fell away, and a gate in the railing swung back across the promenade, while grooms led out of the arena five or six beautiful stallions. The New England college professor had a healthy liking for a fine horse, and his eyes followed these superb creatures till they were out of sight. Then in the clear space at the far end of the building he saw three coaches, one of them already equipped with its four-in-hand, while the horses were being harnessed to the others.

He stood there for a minute or two looking at them with interest. Then he turned his back, and once more began circling about the arena in the thick of the crowd, with no chance of seeing a horse again until he could get to the seat to which his ticket entitled him. He took out the bit of pasteboard and examined it again, and he saw that his place was very near the entrance, only he had gone to the right when he came in instead of to the left. By this time the men and women on exhibition in the boxes had begun to lose the attraction of novelty : and Morton walked on as swiftly as he could make his way through the crowd, wishing to get his seat in time to see the competition of the coaches.

He had come almost to the foot of the little flight of steps by which he could reach his seat when he happened to look up, and he caught sight of a familiar face. In a box only a score of feet before him there sat a lady about whose high-bred beauty there could hardly be two opinions. She was probably nearly thirty years old, but she looked fresher than either of the girls by her side. She wore a costume combining studied simplicity and marked individuality : and yet no one who saw her took thought of her attire, for her beauty subdued all things, and made any adornment she might adopt seem as though it were necessary and inevitable.

There was a suggestion of stiffness in her carriage, and perhaps a hint of haughtiness : but when she smiled she was as charming as she was handsome.

As his eyes first fell upon her Morton's heart gave a sudden thump, and then beat swiftly for a minute or two. Although he had not seen her for nearly ten years, he recognized her instantly. She had changed but little since they had met for the last time. He would have known her anywhere and at once.

And if he had been in any doubt as to her identity, it would have been dispelled by the conversation of the two young men who had

BETWEEN TWO EVENTS

He wondered if he had courage to go up and speak to her. He remembered her so sharply, he recognized every turn of her head and every dainty gesture of her hands, he recalled so distinctly every word of their conversation the last time they met that it did not seem possible to him that she might have forgotten him. And yet it was not impossible. Why should she remember what he could not forget?

While he was hesitating, the party in her box broke up. One of the young ladies who were sitting with her arose and came down the steps, escorted by two young men, and as they passed Morton he caught from their conversation that they were going to the stables below to see a certain famous horse in his stall. The other young lady had changed her seat to the back of the box, where she was deep in conversation with a young man who had taken the chair beside hers. Mrs. Suydam was left alone in the front of the box.

She sat there apparently not bored with her own society, and obviously indifferent to the frank staring of the men and women who passed along the promenade a few feet below her. She sat there calm in her cold beauty, unmoved and uninterested, almost as though her thoughts were far away.

Morton made up his mind, and pressed forward again.

When he was within a yard or two of the steps

leading to her box she happened to glance down, and she caught his eye fixed upon hers. She was about to glance away, when she looked again, and then a smile of recognition lighted her face, followed by the faintest of blushes.

She bowed as Morton raised his hat, and she held out her hand cordially when he climbed the steps to her box.

"I hardly dared to hope that you would remember me, Mrs. Suydam," he said, as he shook hands gently. "It is so long since I saw you last."

"How could you think I should ever forget the pleasant month I spent in your mother's house?" she returned. "We do not have so many pleasant months in life, do we, that we can afford to let any one of them slip out of memory? You haven't forgotten me, have you? Well, then, why should I forget you and your mother and the lovely little college town?"

"That month I can't forget," he responded; "but it was a long while ago, and my existence is uneventful always, while yours is full—and then so many things have happened since."

"Yes," she admitted, "so many things have happened. I'm married, for one thing. But that hasn't made me forget how kind you all were to me. Can't you sit down here for a few minutes and give me all the news of the college and the town?"

"I shall be only too glad," he said, taking the chair by her side. "Where shall I begin?"

14

"Tell me about yourself," she commanded.

"That won't take me long," he returned. "Very little has happened to me. I was going to Germany—perhaps you remember—that fall, after you left us. Well, I went, and I stayed two years, and I took my Ph.D. there, and I came back to the old college, and they gave me a professorship—and that's all."

"That's enough, I think," she answered, looking at him frankly with her dark eyes. "You have your work to do, and you do it. I don't believe there is anything better in life than to be sure what you ought to work at and to be able to work at it."

"I suppose you are right," Morton acknowledged. "I find hard labor is often the best fun, after all. But I can get solid enjoyment out of loafing, too. I don't recall that we worked very steadily that month that you were with us, and we certainly had a very good time. At least I did!"

"And so did I," she declared, unbending a little, and with a laugh of pleasant recollection. "I enjoyed every minute of my visit. I wish I could have such good times now!"

"Don't you?" he asked.

"Not often," she answered. "Perhaps never."

"You surprise me," he replied. "I supposed you were being entertained by day and by night, week in and week out, from one year's end to another."

"So we are," she explained.' "But being entertained isn't always being interested, is it?"

"That's the theory, isn't it?" he rejoined.

"It may be the theory," she confessed, "but I'm sure it isn't the practice."

"I know that little college town of ours is remote from the path of progress," he went on. "but sometimes we behold those messengers of civilization, the New York Sunday newspapers. And whenever I do get one I am certain to see that you have been to a dinner-dance here, to a *bal poudré* there. I should judge that you lived in an endless merry-go-round of gayety."

She smiled again, and there was no sadness in her smile, only a vague, detached weariness. "Dinner-dances are the fashion just now," she said ; "and if there is anything more absurd than the fashion it's to waste one's strength struggling against it."

"That is very end-of-the-century philosophy," he commented.

"It's philosophical not to want to be left out of things, isn't it?" she inquired. "Even if one doesn't care to go, one doesn't like not to be asked, and so one goes often when one would rather stay at home."

"I should think that if many people had motives like that, your parties here in New York might be rather dull," he retorted, with a little laugh.

"They are dull," she returned, calmly. "Sometimes they are very dull. But, of course, it doesn't do not to go."

"I suppose not," he agreed.

"But I find myself wondering sometimes," she continued, "where all the dull people in society were dug up. Sometimes after a long month of dinners I get desperate and almost wish I could renounce the world. Why, at the end of last winter I told my husband that we had not spent a single evening home since we got back from Florida, and we hadn't had a single pleasant evening, not one. He didn't think it was as bad as that, and perhaps it wasn't for him either, for I don't believe the women are as stupid as the men. Of course now and then there was a dinner I thought I should enjoy, but I never did. I'd see the clever man I'd have liked to talk to ; I'd see him far down at the other end of the table, and that was all I did see of him. Some dreary old man would take me in, and then after dinner I'd have perhaps two or three little boys come up and try to pay compliments, and succeed in keeping away the men who might possibly have had something to say."

"And yet yours is the set that so many people seem to be trying so hard to enter," he suggested ; "that is, if I understand aright what I read in New York novels."

"Yes," she answered, "I suppose that's the chief satisfaction we have — we know we are envied by the people who want to visit us, and

MEN AND WOMEN AND HORSES

to have us visit them. I suppose the desire to get
into Society fills the emptiness in many a woman's
life: it gives her something to live for."

"They don't seem to have much of the stern
joy that foemen feel." Morton commented.
"They take life desperately hard. Over there
in the other corner I saw a handsome woman,
and I overheard a man call her by name—she's
the wife of Cyrus Poole, the Wall Street operator. And when I saw the unsatisfied aspiration
in her face, I wondered whether she was one of
those social strugglers I had read about."

"Mrs. Poole?" echoed Mrs. Suydam, indif-
ferently. "I don't know her: I've met her, of
course—one meets everybody—but I don't know
her. She is good-looking, and she is in the thick
of the social struggle. Upward and outward is her
motto—Excelsior! They used to say that all last
winter you could positively hear her climb. But
then they have said that of so many people! She
is clever, they say, and she entertains lavishly, so
I shouldn't wonder if she succeeded sooner or
later: and then she will be so disappointed."

Morton smiled. "From your account," he said,
"the social struggle is rather a tragedy than a
comedy: and I confess it has hitherto struck me
as not without a suggestion of farce."

"It is absurd, isn't it?" she returned, smiling back. "And are we not a very snobbish
lot? Jimmy declares that society in New York
is almost as snobbish as it is in London even."

There was a moment of silence, and then Morton asked, a little stiffly, " How is Mr. Suydam ? You know I have never had the pleasure of meeting him."

" Haven't you ?" Mrs. Suydam responded. " You can see him soon. He's to drive George Western's coach. There they come now !"

A trumpet sounded ; a gate in the railing at the Fourth Avenue end of the building was opened ; and a coach was driven into the arena. A very stout man sat on the box alone.

Mrs. Suydam raised her long-handled eyeglass and looked at the approaching coachman.

" Oh, that's not Jimmy," she said, quickly ; " of course not. That's the man they call The Adipose Deposit."

The trumpet sounded again, and a second coach was turned into the arena. The four horses were beautifully matched bays. The driver was a tall, thin, youngish man, who sat impassible on the box, and gave no sign of annoyance when a wheel of the vehicle rasped the gate-post.

" That's Mr. Suydam," said the lady to whom Morton was talking, as the bays trotted briskly past them, the man on the box holding himself rigidly and handling the ribbons skilfully.

" He is quite a professional," Morton remarked.

" Isn't he ?" Mrs. Suydam replied. " You know he drove the Brighton coach out of London for three years. He really does it very well, they all say. I've told him that if we ever lost our money he would make a very superior coachman."

"Those bays go together admirably," the college professor declared, "and Mr. Suydam handles them superbly. But how pitiful it is to see their tails docked!"

"Oh, they do that in England," she explained, "so it's fashionable. But it is ugly, isn't it? Do you remember what a lovely long tail that Kentucky mare had, the one I rode that day—"

Then Mrs. Suydam paused suddenly.

"Yes," answered Morton, not looking at her, "I remember it."

Mrs. Suydam conquered her slight embarrassment and gave a light little laugh.

"How rude I have been!" she said. "Here I've been talking about myself and about my husband, and I haven't asked about you. Are you married yet?"

"No," he answered, and now he looked at her, and she blushed again; "and I am not likely ever to marry, I think. There was only one woman in the world for me, and I told her so, but she didn't care for me at all, and she told me so—and then she touched up that Kentucky mare and rode away with my heart hanging at her saddle-bow."

"You can find a better woman than she is," was her response; "a woman who will make you a better wife than she would ever have done."

Before Morton could reply to this, the girl and
the two young men who had been in the box at
first returned from their visit to the stables. The
trumpet sounded again, and the judges made the
drivers of the four coaches—for two more had
entered after Mr. Suydam's—repeat their evolu-
tions around the arena. And then, after pro-
tracted consultation together, the awards were
made, and grooms ran to attach rosettes to the
leaders of the team driven by the stout gentleman,
who took the first prize, and then to the leaders
of the team driven by Suydam, who took the second prize. The numbers of the winning coaches
were displayed on the wide sign-boards at each
end of the hall. The coaches were driven around
again, and then out. The trumpets were silent
for a while ; and the brass band crashed forth
again.

"Jimmy won't like not getting the first prize,
will he ?" asked the girl who had just returned
to the box.

"I don't think it will worry him," answered
his wife, with a return of her haughty manner.

She had not introduced Morton to any of the
others in the box.

In the presence of so many it was impossible
to resume their conversation on the old friendly
basis. It seemed to Morton that since the girl
and the young men had come back there was a
difference in Mrs. Suydam's manner towards
him ; he could not define it to himself, but he

A PRIZE-WINNER

felt it. Perhaps she was conscious of this herself.

When he made a movement preparatory to going, she said : " Must you go ? I wanted you to meet my husband. Can't you drop in and lunch with us to-morrow ?"

Morton thanked her and regretted that he might have to take a midnight train, and expressed his pleasure at having met her again. Then she held out her hand once more : and a minute later he was again in the thick of the throng circling along the promenade.

Before he reached the entrance the music was checked suddenly and the trumpet blared out, and then the voice of a man in the centre of the building was heard, intermittently, hopelessly endeavoring to inform the thousands packed in the splendid edifice that the fastest trotter in the world would now be shown. The crowd which was staring steadily at the men and women in the boxes paid little attention to this proclamation : to it the men and women in the boxes were far more interesting than any horses could be, even if any one of these could trot a mile in two minutes without a running mate.

(1895)

In the Watches of the Night

IT was still snowing solidly as the carriage swung out of the side street and went heavily on its way up the avenue; the large flakes soon thickened again upon the huge fur collars of the two men who sat on the box bolt-upright; the flat crystals frosted the windows of the landau so that the trained nurse could see out only on one side. She sat back in the luxurious vehicle. She had on the seat beside her the bag containing her change of raiment; and she wondered, as she always did when she was called unexpectedly to take charge of an unknown case, what manner of house it might be that she was going to enter, and what kind of people she would be forced to associate with in the swift intimacy of the sick-room and for an unknown period. That the patient was wealthy and willing to spend his wealth was obvious — the carriage, the horses, the liveried servants, were evidence enough of this. That his name was Swank she also knew: and she thought that perhaps she had heard about the marriage of a rich old man named Swank to a pretty young wife a year or two ago. That he had been taken sick suddenly, and that the case might be seri-

ous, she had gathered from the note which the doctor had sent to summon her, and which had been brought by the carriage that was now returning with her.

She had ample time for speculation as they drove up the avenue in the early darkness of the last day of the year. The Christmas wreaths still decked the windows of the hotels, although through the steady snow she could see little more than a blur of reddish-yellow light as she sped past. There were few people in the avenue, except as they crossed the broader side streets, now beginning to be filled with the throng of workers returning home after the day's labor. They passed St. Patrick's Cathedral, already encrusted with snow whiter than its stone. They came to Central Park, and they kept on, with its broad meadows on their left gray in the descending darkness. At last the carriage drew up before a house on a corner—a very large house it seemed to the trained nurse; and its marble front struck her as cold, not to call it gloomy. Workmen were hastily erecting the frame of an awning down the marble steps, and a path had been made across the snowy sidewalk.

The footman carried her bag up the stoop and rang the bell for her.

The door was opened promptly by a very British butler.

"This is the nurse for Mr. Swank," said the footman. "Is he any better?"

"'E's about the same, I'm thinkin'," the butler responded. "This way, please," he said to the owner of the bag, which the footman deposited just inside the door. "I'll take you up to Mr. Swank's room, and I'll send your bag up to you afterwards."

The trained nurse followed the butler up the massive wooden stairs, heavy with dark carving. She noticed that the house was now dimly lighted, and that there was a going and a coming of servants, as though in preparation for an entertainment of some sort.

"We 'ave a dinner on this evening," the butler explained; "only twenty-four: but it's 'ard Mr. Swank ain't goin' to be able to come down. We're keepin' the 'ouse dark now, so it won't get too 'ot at dinner-time."

Whatever the reason for the absence of adequate illumination, it made the upper hall even more dismal than the one below—so the trained nurse thought.

"That's Mr. Swank's room there; and 'ere's 'is dressin'-room, that you're to 'ave—so the doctor said," the butler declared, leading the stranger into a small room with a lofty ceiling, and with one window overlooking Central Park. The shades had not been drawn: the single gas-jet was burning dimly: there was no fireplace: and a sofa on one side had had sheets and blankets put on it to serve as her bed.

She almost shivered, the place seemed to her

so cheerless. But her training taught her not to think of her own comfort.

"This will do very well," she asserted.

"I'll tell them to fetch up your bag," the butler said, as he was about to withdraw. "Would you be wantin' any dinner later?"

"Yes," she answered, "I would like something to eat later—whenever it is convenient."

The butler left the room, only to reappear almost immediately.

"'Ere's the doctor now," he announced, holding the door open.

A tall, handsome man, with a masterful mouth, walked in with a soft, firm tread.

"So this is the nurse," he began. "Miss Clement, isn't it? I'm glad you were able to follow my note so quickly. If you will come into the next room, where the patient is, as soon as you have changed your dress, I'll tell you what I wish you to do."

With that he left her; and in less than ten minutes she followed him into the large bedroom on the corner of the house. It was an unusually spacious room, with a high ceiling and four tall windows.

There was a dull-red fire, which seemed insufficient to warm even the elaborate marble mantel. Almost in one corner stood a large bed, with thick curtains draped back from a canopy.

The doctor was sitting by the side of the bed as the nurse came into the room.

"SHE ALMOST SHIVERED, THE PLACE SEEMED TO HER
SO CHEERLESS"

"This is Miss Clement, Mr. Swank," he said, in a cheerful voice, to the old man, who lay in the bed motionless. "She will look after you during the night."

Mr. Swank made no answer, but he opened his eyes and looked at the woman who had come to nurse him. She used to say afterwards that she had never felt before so penetrating a gaze.

The doctor turned to her, and in the same professionally cheery tones he said: "I sent for you, nurse, because Mrs. Swank has an important dinner to-night, and it might therefore be difficult for her to give Mr. Swank the attention he may require."

The physician was addressing the nurse, but it seemed to her that his words were really intended for the patient, whose eyes were still fixed on her.

All at once the sick man sat up in bed and began to cough violently. When the paroxysm had passed he sank back on the pillow again and closed his eyes wearily.

"I think that was not as severe as the last one," the doctor remarked: "I can leave you in Miss Clement's hands now. Perhaps, if I happen to be up this way about midnight, I may drop in again just to see that you are getting on all right. In the mean time, nurse, you will see that he takes these capsules every two hours—he had the last at half-past five. And you will take his temperature every hour if he is awake."

15

He said good-night to Mr. Swank in the same cheering tone, and then he went to the door. The nurse knew that she was to follow him.

When they stood alone in the hall, the doctor said to her : " If there is any change in the pulse or the temperature, send for me at once. Ring for the butler, and tell him I am to be sent for ; he will know what to do. Mr. Swank has influenza only, but his heart is weak, and he needs careful attention. I shall be here again the last thing to-night."

When the nurse returned to the corner room the patient had fallen into a heavy doze, and she took advantage of this to prepare for the long vigil. She arranged her own belongings ready to her hand in the dressing-room set aside for her use. In that room she did not lower the shade, and she even stood at the window for a minute, trying to look out over Central Park, hidden from her by a swaying veil of swirling snow. The workmen had completed the canvas tunnel down the stoop to the edge of the sidewalk, and the lanterns hung inside the frame-work revealed grotesquely its striped contortions. As the nurse gazed down on it an old man without any overcoat sought a temporary shelter from the storm in the mouth of the awning, only to be ordered away almost immediately by the servant in charge.

The nurse went back into the larger room. She looked at her patient asleep in the warm bed. She wondered why life was so unequal ; why the one man should spend the night in the snowy street. while the other had all that money could buy — shelter. warmth, food, attendance. She recalled how her father used to declare that the inequalities we see all around us are superficial only. and that there are compensations. did we but know them, for all deprivations, and that all apparent advantages are to be paid for, somehow. sooner or later. More than ever to - night she doubted the wisdom of her father's saying. How could there be anything but inequality between the old man in the street there below and the old man here in the bed ? The thing seemed to her impossible.

As she became accustomed to the dim light of the room she was able to note that the furniture was heavy and black. that the carpet was unusually thick, that the walls had large paintings hanging on them, that the ceiling was frescoed in sombre tints. On all sides of her she saw the evidences of wealth and of the willingness to spend it : and yet the room and the house seemed to her strangely uninviting. and almost repellent. She asked herself why the sick man lying there asleep in the huge bed had not used his money to better advantage, and had not at least made cheerful his own sick-room. Then she smiled at her own foolishness. Of course the owner of the room had not expected to be stricken down : of course he had no thought of illness when he had furnished.

She moved gently about the room and tried to look at the pictures, but the illumination was insufficient. All that she could make out clearly were the names of the artists carved on tiny tablets attached to the broad frames; and although she knew little about painting, she had read the newspapers enough to be aware that pictures by these artists must have cost a great deal of money—thousands of dollars each, very likely. If she had thousands to spend, she believed that she could lay them out to better advantage than the owner of the house had done here. It struck her again as though the sick man had more than his share of the good things of life. She had not yet heard him speak, and she had not really had a good look at him ; but she could not help thinking that a man who had so much, who had the means of doing so much, who was absolutely his own master, and who could spend a large fortune just as he pleased—she could not help thinking that he ought to be happy. It was true that he was ill now, but the influenza wears itself out at last ; and when he was well he had so much money that he must be happier than other men—far happier than poor men, certainly.

When she came to this conclusion she was standing near the foot of the bed, looking at the man lying there asleep. It was on the stroke of half-past seven, and she had come to let him have his medicine again. Then she noticed that

his eyelids were parted, and that he was looking
at her.

"It is time to take one of these capsules now,"
she said, gently moving to his side and offering
it to him.

He took it without a word, and gulped it down
with a swallow of water.   Then he sank back on
the pillow, only to raise himself at once, as he
was again shaken by a severe fit of coughing.

At last he lay back on the bed once more, still
breathing heavily.

A fresh, young voice was heard at the door leading to the hall, saying, "May I come in, John?"
and then a graceful young figure floated into the
room with a birdlike motion.

The sick man opened his eyes wide as his wife
came near him, and a smile illumined his face.

"How beautiful you are!" he said, faintly,
but proudly.

"Am I?" she answered, laughing a little.   "I
tried to be to-night, because there will be the
smartest women in New York at Mrs. Jimmy
Suydam's dance, and I wanted to be as good as
any of them."

The nurse had withdrawn towards the window
as the wife came forward, and she did not believe
that any woman at Mrs. Jimmy Suydam's, wherever that might be, could well look more beautiful than the one who now stood smiling by the
side of the sick husband.

She was a blonde, this young wife of an old

man, a mere girl, and the vaporous blue dress was cut low on a slender neck girt about by a single strand of large pearls, while a diamond tiara high on her shapely head flashed light into every corner of the darkened sick-room.

"I thought I'd just run in and see how you were before anybody came," she said, lightly. "Dinner is at quarter to eight, you know. I do *wish* you could be down. We shall miss you *dreadfully*. Of course I sent out at the last minute and got a man to fill your place, so we shall sit down with twenty-four all right; but then—"

Here she broke off, having caught sight of the third person in the room.

"So this is the nurse Dr. Cheever sent for?" she went on. "I'm sure she'll take good care of you, John—the doctor is always *so* careful. And if you hadn't had somebody with you I shouldn't have liked to leave you all alone — really I shouldn't!"

With that she circled about the bed again, turning towards the door.

"I must be off now," she explained. "I can't be *wasting* my time on you in this way. I really ought to be down in the drawing-room *now*; and first, I've got to see if the flowers are all right on the table."

Her husband's eyes had followed her wistfully about the room, watching every one of her easy and graceful movements; and when at last she slipped out of the door, it was a moment before he turned an inquiring glance on the nurse, as though to discover what she thought of the brilliant vision.

The nurse came to the side of the bed with her clinical thermometer in her hand.

" You are awake now." she said, with a pleasant smile. " May I take your temperature ?"

Five minutes later, when she was entering in her note-book the high degree shown by the thermometer. and when the patient had again dropped off to sleep. the first guests began to arrive for the wife's dinner party.

The thick snow made the wheels inaudible, but the nurse heard the doors of the carriages slam as those who had been invited passed through the canvas tunnel one after another. In the room next to the dressing-room assigned to her for her own use there was a rustling of silken stuffs. and there were fragments of conversation now and again so loudly pitched as to reach the ear of the young woman who sat silent in the sick-chamber. Then, when all the guests were come, the house sank again into silence. and a tall clock in a corner of the stairs chimed forth the hour of eight.

So long as her patient slept the nurse had little or nothing to do : but though her body was motionless, her thoughts were busy. She was country-bred herself : she had left her home in a little New England village by the sea to make her way in the world. She had now been a

trained nurse for nearly two years; and yet, as
it happened, her work had been either in hotels
or in families of only moderate means. This
was the first time she had been in so handsome
a house or with people of so much wealth. She
could not help being conscious of her surround-
ings, and she caught herself wishing that she too
were rich. She confessed that she would like
to be a guest at the dinner below. She wondered what a dinner-table for twenty-four must be.
To be able to entertain as lavishly as that, and
not to have to worry about the arrangement, or
the cost, or anything — well, that would be an
existence any woman must delight in. She felt
herself capable of expanding, and of being equal
to the enjoyment of any degree of luxury. She
liked her occupation, for she had chosen her own
calling. She had been successful in it too; and
yet she was beginning to be a little afraid that
she had miscalculated her strength. The work
was very laborious and confining, and more than
once of late she had felt overtaxed. It might
be that in a year or two her reserve force would
be exhausted, and she would have to give up the
struggle and go back home, where she would be
welcome, of course, but where she would add to
the burdens her mother was already laden with.

There was an alternative, and never before
had it seemed to her so tempting as when she
was sitting there alone with the sick man in the
darkened corner room of his great house. She

might marry. More than once she had been asked in marriage ; and one man had asked her more than once. He was persistent, and he still declined to accept her refusal as final. He was not an old man yet, although he was twice her age. He was a rich man, even if he was not as wealthy as the owner of the splendid but depressing home where she now sat silently musing. She did not love him, that was true, and there was no doubt about it ; but she did respect him, and she had heard that sometimes love comes after marriage. He could let her have all she longed for, and he was ready to give her everything he had. If she married him she too could have dinners of twenty-four, and wear a rope of pearls and a diamond tiara ; and then, too, she could do so much good with money if she had it.

In the course of her services in the hospital, and afterwards among the poor, she had seen many a case of sore distress which she had been unable to relieve. If she had riches she could accomplish much that was now impossible : she could do good in many ways ; she could relieve suffering and aid the impoverished and help the feeble far more adroitly and skilfully than could any woman who had always been wealthy, and who had not had her experience of life and of its misfortunes and its miseries. She thought that she knew her own character, and she believed that she had strength to withstand the

temptations which beset the rich. Thinking
herself unselfish, she held herself incapable of
keeping for herself alone any good fortune that
might come to her. And she made a solemn
resolve that if she should marry the man who
stood ready to take her to wife she would devote
to good works the greater part of her money and
of her time. She would dress as became her station, of course, and she would entertain sumptu-
ously too ; but no old man should ever be turned
shivering from her door when she was giving a
dinner of twenty-four.

Her revery was interrupted half a dozen times
by the fits of coughing which shook her patient,
and which seemed to her to become more and
more frequent and more violent. At half-past
nine she gave him his medicine again, and took
his temperature once more. Then she made up
the fire, which burned badly ; and she straightened the sheets on his bed, and turned the
pillows.

He soon sank to slumber again, breathing heavily and turning uneasily in his sleep. The house
was singularly still, and no sound of the dinner
party below reached the nurse in the corner room
above. When she happened to go into the dressing-room she found there awaiting her a tray
with several dishes from the dinner table. She
was glad to have something to eat, and she sat
down by the window to enjoy it. The thick, soft
snow had silenced nearly all the usual street

sounds. The carriages that went up and down the avenue were as inaudible as though they were rolling on felt. But sleighing parties became more frequent, and she found a suggestion of pleasant companionship and of human activity in the jingle of the bells. Once a fire-engine sped swiftly past the house, its usual roar deadened by the heavy snow, and its whistle shrilling forth as it neared the side streets, one after another; ten minutes later it came slowly back. The nurse was glad that there was only a false alarm, for she knew how terrible a fire would be in a crowded tenement-house on such a night.

She finished her belated dinner a few minutes after the deep tones of the clock in the hall had told her that it was ten, and that there were left of the old year but two hours more. Except when the sick man waked with a cough, the next hour was wholly eventless.

And yet, when it had drawn to an end, the nurse thought that it would count in her life as important beyond most others, for it was between ten and eleven that she made up her mind to marry the rich man who wanted her for his wife, and whom she did not love. The resolution once determined, she let her mind play about the possibilities of the future. She would not be married till the spring, of course, and they would go to Europe for their wedding-trip. Then, in the fall, she would persuade him to move to New York. He was fond of his own town, but he would get used to the city in time; and they could buy a new house, overlooking Central Park—perhaps in the same neighborhood as the one where she was sitting in the hazy light of the sick-room. She smiled unconsciously as she found herself wondering whether her patient's beautiful young wife would call on her if she purchased the house next door.

It was a little after eleven o'clock when she again heard a rustling of silken stuffs in the room by the side of hers, followed shortly by the voice of the servant in the street below calling the carriages of the departing guests. But some of the diners still lingered, for it was nearly half an hour later before the door of the sick-room opened and the sick man's wife came gliding in again with her languorous grace.

He fixed his eyes upon her at once, and smiled with contentment as she came towards him.

"You've been asleep, haven't you?" she began. "I'm so glad, for of course that's so good for you. We all missed you down-stairs, and everybody asked about you and said they were *so* sorry you were not there. You must hurry up and get well; and I'll give another dinner like this, for it was a *great* success. The flowers were superb—and I don't think any of the women had a handsomer gown than I did. And I know all of them together hadn't as elegant diamonds. I don't believe *anybody* at the dance will have as many either."

"Sit down by me here and tell me all about the dinner," said the sick husband.

"Oh, I can't wait now," the young wife answered. "I *must* be off at once. I've simply *got* to be there in time to see the old year out and the new year in. They say Mrs. Jimmy has a surprise for us, and nobody at dinner had the slightest idea what it *could* possibly be!"

"Are you going to the dance to-night?" asked the man in the bed; and the nurse saw the pleading look in his eyes, even if his wife failed to perceive it.

"Of course I am," was the wife's reply. "I wouldn't miss it for *anything*. I think it's a lovely idea to have a dance on New-Year's Eve, don't you? I *do* wish you were well enough to go, and I'm certain sure Mrs. Jimmy will ask about you—she's always *so* polite. You won't miss me—you will be asleep again in five minutes, won't you?"

"Perhaps," he answered, still clinging to her fingers. "I'll try to sleep."

"That's right," she responded, withdrawing her hand and going towards the door. "I'll trust you to the nurse. She'll take better care of you than I should, I'm afraid. I never was *any* good when people were sick. Now good-bye. I *do* hope you'll be better when I get back. I'll come in and say good-night, of course. I sha'n't be late, either—I'll be home by three—or before four, *anyway.*"

And with that she glided away, smiling back at her husband as she left the room. He followed her with his eyes, and he gazed at the door fixedly after she had gone. There was a hungry look in his face, so it seemed to the nurse, as of one starving in the midst of plenty. With the vain hope that the vision of beauty might yet return, he lay silent, but listening intently, until he heard the sharp slam of the carriage doors. Then he relaxed and turned restlessly in bed.

It was then half-past eleven, and the nurse took his temperature and administered another capsule, as the doctor had ordered. It seemed to her that he was more feverish and that he was coughing more frequently; and even as she saw the patient sink into a broken sleep, she wished that the physician would come soon.

The arrival of the doctor was delayed till a few minutes before midnight, and the nurse had time to reconsider, once and forever, her decision to marry for money and without love. Her mind had been made up slowly and with great deliberation; it was unmade suddenly and unhesitatingly and irrevocably. It was the sight of the mute pleading in the sick man's eyes which made her change her mind. After seeing that look she felt that it would be impossible for her to make a loveless marriage—not for her own sake only, but also for the sake of the man she should marry. If he loved her and she did not love him, there would be no fair exchange : she would be cheating him. When she beheld clearly the meaning of the transaction her honesty revolted. She had refused to marry him more than once, and now her refusal was final.

She stood for a moment at the window and looked out. The snow had ceased falling, and there was already a clearing of the clouds, which let the moonlight pierce them fitfully. The wind blew steadily across the broad meadows of the Park, bending the whitened skeletons of the trees.

Three immense sleighs filled with a joyous and laughing party went down the avenue, bandying songs from one sleigh to the other. A horn was tooted repeatedly in one of the side streets, and there were louder and more frequent whistles from the river craft on both sides of the city. A pistol-shot rang out now and again. It was almost midnight on the last day of the old year; and the new year was to be greeted with the customary chorus of wild noises.

As the nurse turned from the window the doctor entered the room. She made her report briefly, and she told him that the old man's cough was worse, and that he seemed weaker.

While they were standing at the foot of the bed, the patient was seized with another paroxysm. He sat up, shaken by the violent effort —far more violent than any that had preceded it. He seemed to struggle vainly for relief, and then he dropped back limply on the pillows. The physician was at his side instantly, and laid a hand on his heart. There was a moment of silence, and the clock on the stairs began to strike twelve, its chimes mingling with the uproar made by the pistols and the horns and the steam-whistles out-doors.

"That's what I was afraid of," said the doctor at last. "I suspected that he had fatty degeneration of the heart."

"Is he—is he dead?" asked the nurse.

"Yes, he is dead."

But it was not for five or ten minutes that the shrill noises outside ceased.

(1895)

THE END

www.ingramcontent.com/pod-product-compliance
Lightning Source LLC
Chambersburg PA
CBHW030637030726
47497CB00006B/1826